CULTES DES GOULES

also by
Katherine Kerestman

Creepy Cat's Macabre Travels:
Prowling around Haunted Towers,
Crumbling Castles, and Ghoulish Graveyards

also edited by
Katherine Kerestman and S. T. Joshi

The Weird Cat

Shunned Houses:
An Anthology of Weird Stories,
Unspeakable Poems, and Impious Essays

CULTES DES GOULES

KATHERINE KERESTMAN

WordCrafts

Tales included in this volume are fiction. The author has endeavored to be faithful to the times and locations depicted, but all references to persons, places, and events are fictitious or are used fictitiously. Any resemblance to any person, living or dead, is coincidental.

Culte des Goules
Copyright © 2025
Katherine Kerestman

Hardback ISBN: 978-1-967649-20-4
Paperback ISBN: 978-1-967649-21-1

Cover concept and design by Mike Parker.

Published by WordCrafts Press
Cody, Wyoming 82414
www.wordcrafts.net

*"What terrified me will terrify others;
and I need only describe the spectre which had haunted
my midnight pillow."*
~Mary Shelley

Contents

Lethal

Once in a Blue Moon

Her eyes fastened on the window across the small room from her bed, Carolyn hugged her calico cat harder. With no clouds to cover it in the black sky, the full moon blazed with a cold white light, and its beams worked their way in between the crisp white curtains which protected the window. Carolyn pulled her feet up into the bed, but she did not lie down. Amelie squirmed in her arms, but the girl did not release her hold on her furry friend.

The girl's eyes widened as moonlight grew in square feet, crawling along the floor toward her bed, and Carolyn drew herself into a more compact bundle and tried to think of a way out.

She could make a dash for the door, but she would have to try to leap over the moonlight on the floor, a maneuver which would still require passing through the moonbeams which were pouring themselves through the window.

The chilled white light of the moon pooled, mere centimeters from the white eyelet ruffles of the bed skirt. Carolyn slid her fanny back in the bed until her shoulder blades bumped against the wall, maintaining her death grip on Amelie.

She decided the better choice of two dismal alternatives was to escape through the window at her back. She would have to continue her hold on Amelie—and she would have to enshroud them both, from head to toe, in the sheet so the moonlight could not touch them.

She seized a pillow with the hand which was not clutching

the cat, and she shook the foam-filled cushion from out of the pillowcase; and then she pulled the cotton sack over the protesting feline, who registered her opposition to the procedure by inflicting very light scratches upon Carolyn's wrist. Having two hands now, Carolyn reached to the bedside table and grabbed a pair of socks. Quickly pulling them on her bare feet, she tugged the sheet loose from the mattress, where it had been folded in precision hospital corners. She unlocked the other window, the one above her head, and raised the lower pane of glass. Then she covered herself with the sheet. Tucking the mewling pillowcase into the crook of her left arm, she let herself out of the window.

When she had dropped into the dew-slickened clamminess of the lawn, she hugged the side of the house, to hide herself from the observant moon. She found sanctuary in the shade of the eaves hanging above her head.

The sheet she was wearing catching on a rusted nail that was protruding from the siding, Carolyn permitted it to rend a small hole in the fabric that she might see out of it. She sidled along the wall of the house until she reached the downspout at the corner, and then she lowered herself to the ground, and, with one hand maintaining her hold on Amelie and the sheet covering herself, she crept through the cold, wet grass along the base of the shrubbery.

It was not easy moving on her hands and knees while wound in a sheet and carrying a cat-filled pillowcase, but Carolyn resolutely continued her snail-like creeping. She was beginning to yield to an encroaching despair. How was she to escape the all-seeing moon? Where could she go without being seen by the desolate orb?

"Here. Pssst. Here," sounded from the tool shed. At first, Carolyn doubted her ears. When she heard it again, she parted the branches to peer at the shed on the other side of the greenery.

"Who's there?" she whispered.

"Andrew. It's safer here, come over," was the answer. "Crawl under the tarp—it's on the ground on this side of the hedge. I've cut an opening into the back wall of the shed, so you won't have to go into the light."

Carolyn wriggled beneath the tarp and made her way to the shed. She handed her bundle to Andrew, and then he helped her through the opening. Andrew pushed a box in front of the aperture, and then he turned to Carolyn: her head was bent to her knees, and her shoulders shook with her sobbing.

Andrew watched silently until her tears ceased. Carolyn blew her nose and dried her eyes on the dirty sheet, and then she raised her eyes to his. "What's happening?" she groaned.

Gazing steadily into her eyes, he unwrapped Amelie and placed the cat into her arms. Amelie jumped to the floor, curled up beside Carolyn, and began to groom her hind leg, the way cats do when they wish to express a general disgust with things.

Andrew said, "I first had a premonition that something was happening when, on the night of the lunar eclipse—remember that night?—I looked up at the moon. It was a crescent by then, because the shadow of the earth was passing over its face. I was enthralled by the way the shadow played across the speckled whiteness of the moon, and I began taking pictures. Later that night, as I looked at my photos, I noticed a shimmering object above the moon in the picture. I looked at all of the photos. The object was in all of them, and it moved toward the moon, and then circled it, leaving streaks of light in the opaque blackness of the sky. I had not seen the object when I was looking at the moon—at the time, I saw nothing except the moon, and its waxing penumbra. What was the bright, moving object? And why hadn't I seen it while I was studying the moon and the spread of the earth's shadow upon its features?"

Carolyn sadly shook her head.

"I knew something was not right," he continued, "I just sensed it. I showed the pictures to a friend, and he told me to send them to a UFO organization—or maybe sell it to CNN. Logic told me that it was probably an ordinary astronomical event—like a meteor—but I *felt* that it was not a good thing.

"Then all kinds of weird things began to happen—you know, about a month ago. The tides in the oceans got all out of synch, and tsunamis were occurring on ocean shores worldwide, followed by flooding, tornadoes, and power outages. Everyone was evacuating coastal and low-lying areas—literally taking to the hills. You know how people were defending their homes in the higher elevations with guns and makeshift booby-traps.

"'Pregnant women started losing their babies—all kinds of mammals suffered spontaneous abortions. Fish washed up from the oceans, their carcasses covering the beaches.

"And now the days are growing shorter day by day—even though it is springtime. We have only two hours of sunlight each day now. Soon we'll probably have none. And most plant life will die." He bowed his head and folded his hands.

"Do you still think it was only a meteor?" she asked. "And what about all the people who die when the moonbeams touch their skin?"

"It'll be sunlight in a few minutes, I think. We'll have approximately two hours to gather food and supplies, and then we'll have to hide again. There's a can of gas in here. Let's take the car to a store, or a food pantry at a church, or raid a garden for vegetables. We'd better wait until later to talk anymore."

"Okay," she said. "Let's come back to my house after."

"Good as any. Let's make sure Amelie can't get out of here while we're gone. We'll get a lot of food for her, too. I need to take some of the tools from this shed, and nails—oh, there's a pile of plywood. I'll cover your windows good and tight when we get back."

The Walmart looked like it had been hit by a bomb. Shelves were knocked over, and paper was strewn in every direction. There was no electricity, and the refrigerated departments smelled like rotting flesh, rancid food and mold being the daily specials. Carolyn had an idea where the housewares department was located, and in the darkness she was able to find candles and fireplace matches. Lighting a candle to illuminate their scavenging, she loaded her a cart with more candles and matches, and then she filled the remaining space in the cart with whatever residual foodstuffs remained on the emptied shelves, while Andrew filled a second cart with hardware. Then they filled two more carts with nonperishables.

"We have to hurry, we need to get to your house before the moon rises," he said as they pushed the carts to the entrance. "I'll bring the car up to the door."

They had just loaded the last items from their carts into Carolyn's car when a dented grey van pulled up behind them and three men with shotguns emerged from it. Shoving Carolyn into the passenger seat, Andrew slammed the door shut, and ran around the front end of the vehicle to the driver's side. Several bullets struck the trunk as they squealed out of the parking lot. Andrew drove into a wooded park, where he pulled the car onto a wide pedestrian path, hoping to conceal it, in case those men had followed them. Thirty minutes later, when nothing had happened, they returned to Carolyn's house.

For thirty-seven weeks they lived like this. Their world had become an eternal night, for the sun had expired, and they dared not leave the house when the moon was shining. Occasionally, on their foraging expeditions, they would spot other people, who were usually scavenging too, but they kept to themselves, seeking concealment in the darkness. Shrouded from crown to foot to avoid the moonlight, they would occasionally come across peoples' bodies in various states of decay, and they would wonder if those people had been killed by the moon. It could have been starvation, disease, or death at the hands of people like those men they had met at Walmart.

They grew closer. They had known each other before, but only as nodding acquaintances. Over the months they came to depend upon each other, and they formed a little family. One day they lay upon the bed, their arms around each other, speculating upon the photos Andrew had taken during the lunar eclipse in the early spring. Now, in what should have been autumn, only most of the plant life had been drying and decaying for weeks now, and there was no harvest, Andrew was saying that he should have sent his photos to UFO groups or to CNN. Maybe someone would have known what that bright, moving object was. Maybe they could have warned the world. Maybe it wouldn't have mattered if they had, maybe they never stood a chance anyway.

As they lay there talking, Amelie was busy doing something. They heard her scratching and scraping, being a busy little girl. But neither Carolyn nor Andrew possessed the energy to play games with her. Carolyn cooed to her, "Hi, Amelie. Mommy loves you," but she did not stir from the shelter of Andrew's arms. After a while, though, Carolyn sat up to stretch, on her way to the kitchen to prepare their simple meal. She smiled to see Amelie chasing a moonbeam stretching across the floor—and then—*realizing*—she screamed.

"Andrew—Andrew—she pried it open—the board on the window—the moon's coming in!"

He sprang from the bed, striving to avoid the moonlight while he crammed the plywood back into its position in the window. That done, he dropped onto the couch and sat with his elbows on his knees and his head in his hands. Carolyn sat next to him. For many minutes, they sat there without speaking.

"Maybe everything will be fine. It was only a crack, very little moonlight came in. I'd better get back to opening cans."

As they were sitting at the table eating their Boston baked beans, they heard Amelie retching. Carolyn knocked over her chair—as she jumped up from the table to run to the living room— Amelie was painfully hunched over, stretching her neck in an effort to evacuate the offending substances from her gut. Carolyn sat upon the floor by her baby, lightly stroking her damp fur, telling her it would be all right, her mom and dad were with her and they loved her, and she would get better. Weakly, Amelie nudged

Carolyn's hand with the top of her head, which seemed to use up all her strength, and then, with a shudder, she rolled onto her side and stopped breathing.

Andrew held Carolyn tight. "Don't ever let me go," she told him, "Don't leave me. Oh, poor Amelie, poor, beautiful Amelie," and he held her as tight as he could all through the night.

After they had slept—they didn't know if it was morning or night, now, with no sunrises anymore—and woke up, Andrew dug a hole under the bushes and Carolyn placed Amelie into it. When they returned inside, Andrew asked her for her almanac. He wanted to see what the phase of the moon would be:

"Maybe if we keep a diary of what happens and correlate it with the phase of the moon, we might learn something useful."

Over the next week, they made a science of it, searching for clues to the new powers of the moon, whether its toxicity waxed or waned with its cycle, hoping to find at least some way of defending themselves.

"What's the matter, honey," Carolyn asked, attempting to sound cheerful, but with a quavering in her voice. "You look tired." Andrew had been losing weight, which she ascribed to their subsistence diet, and he was becoming very pale. Today he looked feeble as a kitten.

"I have to make a run for some food tomorrow. I think there's a root cellar under that farmhouse in the next town that no one has lived in for a very long time. I'll be fine, don't worry so much," he replied, and he pulled her close and kissed her on the lips. "It's probably just lack of fresh air and exercise. I'm not as buff as I used to be, that's all," and he made her giggle.

"Tonight is the night of the Blue Moon—you know, Carolyn, as in *once in a blue moon*."

"Let's see if I remember correctly—that's the second full moon in a month," she said. "Do I get a gold star, Teacher?" He gave her another kiss. She laid her head upon his shoulder and stroked his hair, and they stood like that for a long time.

When the house began to vibrate, they sprang apart—dishes crashed from the kitchen counter to the floor, and the almanac fell from the kitchen table—they had to hold onto the back of the couch to maintain their balance.

"I'm going outside."

"I'm coming with you."

"No sense in both of us, Carolyn. Help me cover myself up."

Carolyn tucked Andrew tightly in bed linens, and gave him mittens for his hands—sunglasses for his eyes. He got down to the floor and stuck his head out the human-size doggy door he had built for them, so that they would not have to always exit from the same side of the house and could exit on the side least likely to incur the vengeance of the moon.

"My God!" he exclaimed. "Everything is glowing, like fluorescent or something. I'm heading for the hedges to get under them and have a look."

"Please, don't go," she cried.

"I have to see what's happening, honey," he said as he wriggled out the hole. He called to her, "Carolyn, the sky's full of them. Bright, moving objects, forming a halo around the moon. Stay inside."

The house began to quiver even more, and Carolyn had difficulty remaining in a kneeling position by the escape hole.

"Come back, Please!"

"They're coming closer. *Fast!* They're coming here. They're—landing! *Right here!*"

The vibrations knocked Carolyn off her knees. As she lay there, she gripped the floor, as if she would be shaken off of it. Pulling herself back on her knees, she looked out of the hole.

"I'm coming back," Andrew cried. "Here I come. Oh, God, what are they? Why didn't I tell anyone about my pic—"

"Andrew? Andrew. Andrew!" Carolyn screamed, as Andrew collapsed outside the manhole. His hand was cold. Blood was streaming from his mouth, his nose, his eyes.

She drew back from the opening and threw up.

She got up and went to the bedroom, where she picked up Andrew's revolver from the nightstand. She returned to the small door he had built for them, and she lay down before it. With her left hand, she reached through the opening to touch his face. With her right hand, she pulled the trigger.

The Silvery Lethal Moon

"H urry, Steven," she whispered, scanning the darkness around them. She moved closer to him. "Can you jimmy the window? I'm so glad the sky is overcast. There may be a storm coming, but at least there's no moon. Still, we could get caught."

"It's getting looser—I think I'll have it open in a minute."

Amy leaned against the red bricks of the Westville High School building, trying not to remember the time when she was a student there. When she sat at a desk, distracted by the traffic on the street outside the window, needing to force her attention back to the trigonometry problem in her textbook. When she ate her bag lunch on the lawn in the nice spring weather that preceded summer break. She turned to observe Steven's work at the window: "You did it!"

He took her hand and pulled her to his side. Together, they pushed the sticky window open. They took turns climbing inside the basement of the shuttered school, and then they pulled the flashlights from their hoodies.

Steve told her, "We've got to find the storage closets. Where do you think we should start?"

"I'll bet there's an orientation brochure with a map in the reception area. Let's look there. I'm sure we'll find lots of closets in the halls, gymnasium, band and locker rooms, too."

"Okay. We'll start at the office, and then work our way down the halls."

An hour later, after Steven had broken through many locked doors, in the band room they found what they had come for: black graduation gowns. Yards and yards of opaque black fabric. They loaded them into trash bags and boxes, and they dragged them to the basement window. Steven boosted Amy out the window, and then he handed her their booty through the opening. When the last bag had gone through the window, Steven climbed out. The pair filled the car they had come in, a marine-blue PT cruiser they had found a few months ago, the keys in the ignition, a rotted corpse in the driver's seat, and then they went home.

The next day, while Steven tacked black fabric over all the windows of the house, Amy fashioned hooded cloaks in their sizes from the pomp and circumstance. They had already obtained ski masks and leather gloves from the sports department at a big-box store.

"This is good," said Amy, "but hot—oh, I almost forgot how cold it is outside now—I almost forgot that the sun is gone. Funny, how you can forget that things are not the same anymore."

"Good job, Amy. We'll be well-protected now. We make a good team."

"I'm afraid it won't be good enough. How many people have we seen die?"

"By surviving so long, we've learned a few things that they didn't know. We'll manage."

"We need light bulbs, batteries—and lanterns, if we can find them."

"Steven, I've been wondering if anyone has ransacked the Boy Scout camp in Frederick County—you know, the one that's out in no-man's-land where country meets wilderness?"

"Let's check it out. Put your protective clothing on. And don't forget your gloves. Be sure there is no skin that is uncovered—there is never a time without any moonlight."

"You mean our couture moonbeam cloaks—designed and tailored by yours truly?"

"That I do. After you, Amy."

"How much longer do you think, Steven?"

"Oh, another thirty, forty minutes. We can't drive too fast in the dark. It makes me nervous, driving out in the middle of nowhere—who knows who's watching our headlights?"

"I know." Amy looked down, staring at her gloved hands by the dashboard light. "It's been so long since the sun went away—six months, I think."

"Eight."

When their high-beams illuminated the Camp Wilderness sign, Amy squeezed Steven's shoulder. They drove the long, undulating drive from the rural highway into the woods. In the near-total darkness, they could see nothing except the occasional white sign which indicated Registration, Cabins, Pool, Lake, Dining Hall, with arrows pointing in their various directions. They had chosen this night for the extensive cloud cover, which blocked nearly all the light from the sliver of the lethal moon.

"I never used to appreciate clouds," said Amy. "They are some of our best protection when we go outside now. On a cloudless day, we can't even leave the house anymore."

"A crescent moon is the best opportunity we'll get—a crescent moon with an overcast sky. We've got to make the most of it. Here we are. The Administration Building. The Mess Hall's in the same building."

"Let's start in the maintenance storeroom and then go to the pantry. It looks like we're the first ones here!" They filled the cruiser with as much as it could hold—shoving their plunder under the seats and in the glove box, and they tied boxes to the roof of the car. Afterward, they dined on cans of Spaghetti-o's and lemonade at the mess hall table, and canned pudding for dessert. Then they returned to the car.

When they were about halfway back to Westville, Steven

said to his nodding companion, "Amy. Amy, there's a car behind us. See the lights?"

"We have to lose them, Steven. We don't know who they are. It's starting to rain."

"Amy, I think I can lose them at the road that goes down into the hollow. It snakes around, and if I can get out of their view for a minute, I can hide the car under a bridge—there are two bridges that cross that creek—or maybe behind a cabin."

"Okay."

Steve depressed the accelerator, increasing their speed to about 40 mph. The car behind them went faster, too. As soon as he saw the sign for the winding road, Steven made a sharp left and followed the tortuous road as fast as he dared in the dark. The other car kept going in a straight line.

"They'll probably turn around and come for us."

"Steven—that sign says cabins coming up—on the right."

"Okay. I'll go that way. We need to find a place to shelter and cut the lights. Hold on, the road's coming up." He cut a sharp right turn.

"Over there, Steven—the sign says there are hiking trails. Can we drive on them?"

"We shall see. There's a fenced-in area—probably restrooms. I'll park behind there and then go dark."

After hiding out several hours, they returned to the road and made it home without encountering any other cars. They brought their provisions into the house and parked the car in the garage.

"Do you think it's morning or night? I guess it really doesn't matter anymore."

"What matters is that the days are getting colder, Amy. That's what I'm worried about."

"Have you talked with anyone lately about the strange lights in the sky?"

"No one since we both talked with the couple we met at the supermarket in Lawrencetown, when we got the charcoal and the grill and the kerosene, a couple of months ago. Neither of us gets to socialize much these days."

"I guess there's no sense in hitting up the After Five dresses at the department store, then. Seriously, though, what's with the moving lights in the sky—do you still think they're UFOs?"

"You know as well as I do, that they probably are. It's stopped raining. I don't hear the rain hitting the roof anymore. I'm going out to get the water buckets and barrels and bring them inside. Help me into my designer cloak, Miss von Furstenberg."

"Here's your sunglasses. I'll open the door for you. Bye." Amy closed the door and waited to hear Steven's voice.

"Open up," he said. Amy opened the door and helped him push the barrel into the living room. Steven went back outside, and she closed the door behind him. She was awaiting his return with the thirteenth container of water, when Steven shouted, "Open the door, Amy!"

He tumbled inside the door, dropping the bucket of rainwater on the porch stoop—and then he locked the door, shouting, "Slide that table over here, Amy. *Quick!*" and she did so.

"What's wrong, Steven?" she asked, frightened.

"It *was* UFOs. There's one of them across the street—behind the red barn. I saw something glinting in the moonlight. I couldn't really make out what it was through these damned peepholes in my lenses, so I crawled over there."

"Oh, Steve, that's so dangerous."

"I covered myself with a tarp—I put it over my moonbeam cloak. When I got across the road, I saw that it was a large metal machine. A spaceship, I guess. It was glowing a soft green in the moonlight. I got back as fast as I could, wrapped up in all these damned layers."

"Steven. Oh, no! I'm so glad you're back safe," and they embraced, as if they sought by that means to stop their trembling.

The small house started to vibrate, and water splashed from the buckets, wetting the carpet. Crockery in the kitchen fell from the shelves onto the tile floor, becoming a pile of porcelain shards. Amy and Steven let go of each other and held onto the furniture instead to keep from falling. Sounds of glass breaking and books thumping to the floor filled the house—along with a churning, humming sound in an unfamiliar key. Steven drew Amy to a corner of the room and pulled her down behind the sofa. Plaster falling from the ceiling powdered their hair. When the mantel crashed from the fireplace, they turned their heads that way—and they saw that the hearth was aglow with a green incandescence.

Amy turned to Steven and buried her face in his chest. He whispered into her ear, "Get your moonbeam cloak."

"It's right here—on the sofa."

She reached for the cloak and pulled it over her head. They could not see each other's faces anymore.

"I guess we have to make a run for it," whispered Amy.

"I don't think we're safe in here," agreed Steven, kissing the top of her head through the two layers of black gabardine. "Don't let that moonlight touch you. Amy, I couldn't stand it if anything happened to you."

"I won't, Steven. I love you."

Steven pulled the door open. Amy stepped out into the moonlight, and he followed, picking up the tarp, which he had discarded at the door, and throwing it over the both of them; and they ran to the garage, which was plainly visible now by the ivory luminosity of the lethal moon, unfiltered in the cloudless and starry firmament.

When they reached the shed, which was halfway between the house and the garage, Amy thrust Steven to the ground. She spoke through the fabric into his ear:

"There's something over there."

Through the pinpoint holes in their cloaks, all they could see was a green glimmering, a shapeless mass that seemed to be moving toward them. Steven pulled her gloved hand:

"Let's get out of here," he cried, dragging her toward the garage. And then he lost his balance—teetered backward. Amy screamed. Steven's cloak was being pulled from his head! He managed to preserve his hold on Amy's hand; seconds later, though, he was overcome by weakness—and he buckled. As Amy was trying to understand what was happening to Steven, she observed one of the green-glowing beings standing over him—it was holding Steven's cloak, and Steven, illuminated by the wan light of the moon—was lying in a crumpled heap. Blood was flowing from his mouth. She moved to help him—but she was wrenched back by a powerful limb, and she found herself being lifted off her feet and carried across the yard before she lost consciousness.

The iridescent alien bore her flaccid body to the strange craft which had landed next to their house. A sliding panel opened in its glowing surface, and the creature bore her inside.

Project Diana

Alan grabbed her tiny wrists, and Midge started kicking his shins. She opened her mouth wide, baring her teeth, and howled—and then she tried to bite his arm, but he tightened his hold on her wrists and held her from him at arm's length.

"Midge, honey. Stop it, baby. Come on now," he spoke soothingly.

"I'm leaving! I've had it! A goddam year!"

"Baby," he replied, broken-hearted.

Sobbing, Midge dropped to her knees. Alan released her wrists and sank to the floor with her. Embracing her shaking body, he sobbed with her.

"A year in this basement, Alan. A whole year! No people. No restaurants or movies or stores. No grass. No fresh air. No sunlight—no, never again. Only darkness. And four goddam concrete basement walls. I can't do this anymore."

"Maybe we should try to find some other people. A new place. There have to be more people left than us."

"Oh, Alan. I know it's not safe to go out there. I don't want to leave you—but I can't ask you to risk everything either. I'm going by myself. I don't want to leave you—but I can't take it anymore! Hiding is not living."

Alan nodded. He kissed a tear from her cheek and whispered in her ear: "I know. I keep thinking about how, twenty years ago, in our parents' time, mass suicide resulted after years of house arrest.

People were afraid of a virus then—COVID, I think. A cold germ that was slightly more lethal than the flu. They shut down the country and locked everyone in their houses. When people tried to resist, they brainwashed them—oh, yeah, it was called *social media*. They learned how to make people think black was white and obedience was freedom."

Midge blew her nose and said, "I remember learning about that in grade school—that's when The Patriarch replaced the old U.S. government, and a lot of other governments in the world. The Patriarch said that the old governments could not keep the people safe from germs, wars, and natural disasters—and the people voted to replace the old government with the Patriarch. And the Patriarch just did the same old things."

"Yes, that's when the suicides started. People jumped from roofs. A lot of them shot their families and then themselves. Some people rented ferries and filled them with passengers, and then shot up the hulls so that they would sink. They left notes saying that they could not live confined and separated. They were tired of taking orders. My parents died in the garage with their car running—and yours were shot by the Patriarchal Police trying to escape into the mountains. A lot of kids ended up in orphanages the way we did."

"Alan, I'm at that point too. I love you—you have given me reason to go on for the last two years—but I cannot live the rest of my life hiding in this basement. You have to let me go. Oh, God! I hate to leave you alone! But I cannot go on hiding until I'm found!" She turned her face from him and gazed at the damp grey wall.

"I'll go with you, then," he spoke, nuzzling his beard against her cheek. "It's not fair of me to keep you in a cage. I love you, Midge, and I don't want to lose you. But you are right—we can't go on indefinitely this way. After we get some sleep, we can start loading the car with as much as we can carry."

"I'll start packing food and clothes and our black capes and hoods. Why don't you get the water from the storeroom."

"Let's get some shuteye, and then we'll get started. We'll face the dark new world together."

"Maybe we'll find we aren't alone. Maybe some other people know a better way to live with the moonlight—it's been a year since we talked to other people."

"Midge, just promise me you won't let the moonlight touch you. I would die," he moaned.

"I won't, Alan. We must be very, very careful."

Two Years Earlier

"That was superb! I'm so glad we came here for our honeymoon," Midge gushed, practically skipping along the sidewalk, her hand on her new husband's arm. "Shaw's *Joan of Arc* is a tour-deforce story of the individual standing up to corrupt institutions."

"And she was burned alive for it," Alan reminded her.

"So sad. And the lawyers and the Church—they just kept twisting things to convict her. They were just making an example of her because she was a woman and a commoner who had stepped out of her station: they had no moral convictions."

"Let's see. Which play shall we see tomorrow? I vote for *The Importance of Being Earnest.*"

They were studying the marquee at one of the theaters at Niagara-on-the-Lake; they had enjoyed a day at Niagara Falls, a good portion of which they had spent leaning upon the rails, mesmerized by the power of the water surging over the cliffs and the immense cloud of mist which rose up from the river and travelled away on the currents of air overhead. They continued their walk along the boulevard of the Edwardian village, which was sweetly scented with the flower beds that filled the median, wet with the gentle dew of the warm evening.

"Here we are, My Lady, our restaurant. I have reserved, for your pleasure, a table on the patio. Look yonder, our champagne is chilling in the bucket." The maître d' arrived to escort the new-lyweds to their table; Midge was delighted with the restaurant which Alan had chosen for them. They had just begun to enjoy their delicious meals when the sky began to glow with beautiful points of light.

"Look at the sky, Alan. Shooting stars!" Midge exclaimed, sipping her champagne from a stemmed goblet. "Wait—the stars are moving in circles! Wait—they're not falling! They're *not stars!*"

"They're circling the moon, Midge. What the heck? They're some kind of aircraft—have to be."

"We'll have to ask the server when he returns. Perhaps he knows what those lights are. Maybe it's the Royal Canadian Air Force. This mushroom ravioli is unbelievable! Oh, look, Alan, that man needs help!"

He turned around to look at the man at the table behind him, who had fallen from his chair to the flagstones. The restaurant staff were already at his side, holding napkins to his face, and the linens were crimson with blood; an ambulance was wailing its way to help him. After the man had been taken away on a stretcher, his stunned wife weeping in the arms of the maître d', the honeymooners had lost their desire to celebrate. They walked back to their hotel, their dinners barely tasted.

Fifteen minutes later, as they were standing in the lobby of The Duchesse, waiting for an elevator to convey them to their room on the second floor, they heard a bloodcurdling scream which seemed to come from the direction of the cocktail lounge. They hurried there to see if they could be of assistance. When they reached the bar, they saw a woman splayed on the ground, just beyond the open doors of the outdoor verandah, on the far side of the intimate room. Blood was running from her nose and eyes, coloring her strand of pearls red. Mystified patrons were milling around her.

"We're going home—now," Alan stated as he pulled Midge toward the elevator. "Pack up. I'll pay the bill and bring the car to the door. Please hurry."

He went out through the revolving door, while Midge entered the elevator.

By sunrise, the couple were travelling the two-lane highway, approaching their home in Lancaster County, Pennsylvania. A bright azure sky complimented the rolling green hills before them, and the horizon, infrequently blemished by buildings, appeared to continue toward infinity. As it ascended to its place in the heavens, the sun shone a cheery golden yellow, and the man and wife began to experience a reprieve from the horrors of the night. They pulled into their driveway, and Midge asked Alan whether he recalled the last time he had seen another car on the road. Alan shifted the gear to park and turned to her:

"I don't remember seeing another car since we crossed the border," he replied, dumbfounded. They grew silent, as electric currents of alarm deployed S.O.S.s throughout their nervous systems. There should have been *some* traffic at this time of the day—their neighbors leaving for work—and the trash containers lining the street should have been picked up the day before. Numbly, they opened their doors. Alan said that he was going across the street to check on his friend Ken, whose car was still in the driveway—Ken would usually have left for work by this time. Midge nodded, watching her husband cross the street. Alan knocked on the front door of his friend's home, and then he pushed through the bushes to look in the front window. He waved at Midge, and then he walked around the corner to the back of the house, disappearing from her sight. A moment later, though, he was sprinting across the road, back to her.

"Ken's dead—blood running from his nose and ears! Let's get what we need from the house and get out of here! Something awful is happening!"

They entered their home and came back out carrying armfuls of necessities: food and water, warm clothing—and their handguns and all the ammunition they possessed. Midge gazed sadly upon the home she was abandoning.

"It's getting cold, Alan. Look at the sky—the sun is already past the midpoint, though it is not yet noon! Is the sun going to set so *early*? I'm going back inside for some blankets."

They turned their car southward, toward Maryland. Every thirty or sixty minutes they would see another car on the road, but none responded to their efforts to flag them down. They topped off their gas tank at an abandoned Sunoco and breakfasted on the perishable food they found there. Near the state line, they turned into another service station, having observed from the road a utility vehicle at the gas pump. Pulling his SUV next to the truck, Alan rolled down his window to speak to a man dressed in coveralls who was filling his tank; several gas cans were lined up next to the truck.

"Get out of here now, before you and your lady get hurt," the man said, replacing the nozzle into the dispenser. He pulled a shotgun from his car, making his intention pretty clear. Alan kept on going.

A Year Later

"This house has been abandoned for months. All the neighbors have gone. The businesses in the area have been ransacked already, and we are in the boondocks. I think it's a good place to hole up."

Alan concurred with Midge's assessment. Maybe they had finally found a safe place to call home.

"No need to hang curtains in our new home—there are no windows in the basement. That's one of the reasons it might be safe here."

"And we can make runs for supplies; and now we have a place to store them besides our car."

They kissed, and then Alan swept Midge from her feet to carry her over the threshold. At first, it was pleasant to make a home in the basement. There was cleaning to do and furniture to lug downstairs from the vacant farmhouse. Alan secured the doors, upstairs and down, using the materials he had discovered in the former occupant's workshop.

Every time they ventured above ground to scavenge or to remove their refuse, which they always buried in the shrubbery, they found evidence of sudden death by hemorrhage, or by violence: there were bodies everywhere. The first time they had beheld firsthand the lethality of the moonlight (since that horrible day in Ontario), they had run for cover, ducking into a toolshed, whose padlock had already been picked. They had been enjoying a rare conversation, with an elderly man named Harold in a deserted wholesale club near a freeway exit—they had discovered each other there, rooting for any remaining food, flashlights, and fuel—and for the sake of companionship, they were combing the aisles and the store-rooms together. Midge and Alan had secreted their vehicle in a small grove of trees adjacent to the parking lot prior entering the big box building; usually, they filled several carts or pallets, rolled them to the door, and then drove their car around to load it. This time, as the trio were nearing the front entrance with their carts, they observed an army surplus vehicle entering the parking lot. Half a dozen boisterous men were standing in the bed of the truck, and they were carrying rifles. Frightened, Harold forgot his provisions and darted out the front door without first covering himself—it was not always easy to remember that each day was shorter than its predecessor, and that the moon might be out at any hour now—and the rays of the moon lighted upon the old man's face. With a loud cry, he toppled forward onto the pavement, and his blood made a puddle around his body. Alan and Midge gasped. He told her to grab a cart, and running, they pushed their carts into a tool shed that was part of a display near the garden department of the store, and then they closed the double doors and held them shut. They held their breaths for much of the next hour, after which Alan crept out to surveille the situation. Finding that the men had gone, the couple pushed their carts to the rear door and brought their car around, carefully swathing every centimeter of their skin before exiting the store. They mourned Harold, as they drove home, for he was their first friend in a year.

For another year, they hid from the moon, and they hid from their fellow survivors. They endured in their basement. Sometimes they plundered a new book to read, or a new board game to play. The months grew long, the daylight eventually disappearing altogether; they never knew what had happened to the sun. It was always night now, and it was always cold. When the electricity and gas failed, they resorted to a wood burning stove, despite the risk of the smoke being seen, for they had no other option. Both of them, but Midge, mostly, became weary of hiding and of the want of human interaction.

She could not help herself. She felt awful, disloyal, but she could not abide her prison anymore. At times she was catatonic, curling up on her mattress in despair, not answering her husband's desperate entreaties. At other times, she was manic—cleaning their prison like a mad fiend, rearranging the spartan furnishings, bustling until she used up all her contained will to live rather than only exist. She yearned for her barely begun career as a high school English teacher, for travel, for academic conferences, birthday parties and rock concerts. Everything was gone, everything but finding food and firewood and avoiding discovery. She knew what was happening to herself, but she could not arrest the ravages wrought by despair and isolation. Over the course of two years, Alan had borne witness to her disintegration, powerless to do more than love her; he was losing the love of his life.

The Present

"Well, husband of mine, at the very least, we shall have a new prison cell. It's better than no variety at all. I do love you, Alan, with all my being. Thank you for taking me out of there."

"You are all I have, Midge—even before the world fell apart. I'll do anything for you."

They grew silent as they drove the backroads, which were unlit and, thankfully, void of other travellers. Swaddled in their black capes and hoods to protect their skin from the deadly light of the moon, they were unable to see each other. There was a half-moon that day, and it seemed to them that the half-moons were bigger now than they used to be, especially since there was no longer a sun with which to compare them. The vegetation was dying, for lack of sunlight and warmth; although the surface of the earth was perpetually frosted now, they both assumed that its interior was still molten, but what did that matter, anyway? Alan stretched his arm, to place his gloved hand on Midge's veiled neck, and she leaned into him. They had no plan—both were simply looking out of their windows into the pale moonlit night, seeking a new haven. They were hoping to find a community of survivors like themselves, or at least a new refuge, where they could shelter from the moon-light, and from the marauders. Wrapped in their own thoughts, they looked silently, left and right, and before them. Both felt an unwanted tear or two trickling from their eyes, but neither lifted a hand to brush it away, each desiring not to sadden the other.

Midge hit the dashboard—and she cried out, as her husband spun the car around, squealing the tires. She clung to the door and to the dashboard to maintain her balance—

"Alan, what's the matter?" she pleaded.

His teeth clenched. He did not answer. He floored the gas pedal instead, taking them as fast as he could in the opposite direction.

"Alan—" she repeated.

"A road block!" he answered.

Midge looked out the rear window—headlights were visible on the road behind them. She turned to face her husband—and she saw headlights coming toward them from the front. Alan swerved from the road—drove into a field of rotten cornstalks. The vehicles closed in—pulled in front of their SUV, so that Alan had to brake to avoid a collision.

"Run!" he yelled to Midge—and a soldier in a Patriarchal Police uniform hit him from behind with a billy club. Midge ran —unaware that her husband was down. The Policeman yanked the protective covering from Alan, exposing him to the light of the moon.

Midge spun when she heard her husband's anguished cry. By the headlights of the military vehicle, she saw that her husband lay—*uncovered*—on the ground. She turned again to flee and ran straight into the arms of a policeman, who lifted her and threw her over his shoulder.

Over her own demented screams she was able to hear him say, "We have another female specimen for Project Diana. Notify Dispatch to rendezvous at Space Vessel One docking site. Over."

She shrieked into the moon-defiled night, and the soulless man in the moon seemed to grin at her performance.

Obedience is Safety is Freedom

The loudspeakers were blaring, "Get your vaccination now. The line forms at the Stadium." The electric billboards in Times Square were scrolling, "The Patriarch Requires Immediate Vaccination of all Citizens" and "The Patriarch Will Keep Us Safe. Obedience is Safety is Freedom." The neon letters were revolving around the brightly lit boards, chugging as a train might which was carrying prisoners to a detention camp, on a circular track of no return. Uniformed Police were blowing their whistles, to keep the line moving.

Masses of people, whose elbows were pushing into other people's backs and sides, and whose backs and sides were being pushed into by other people's elbows, were being crammed by the force of the mass into the doors of the stadium. A few had fallen and were being trampled, but not very many, for they were so tightly packed together it was impossible for most of them to fall, much less to move away.

Alice had just come up the stairs from the subway. She looked back—Jessica was three or four people behind her on the staircase. Alice held her ground in the rush of people at the street-level doorway, and she grabbed Jessica's hand as her friend was being swept past her, by the onrushing crowd. Tightening her grip on her friend's hand, she pulled her to the side, and then around the corner of Grand Central Station, into the nearest alley.

"I just don't trust it. It doesn't feel right. I know the Patriarch is supposed to be our Protector, but it just doesn't add up. Where are all the guys we know? I haven't seen Jim or Tom—or even Michael—in a couple of weeks. Everywhere I go, it seems it's just us girls, anymore. Some of my girlfriends have dropped off the radar, too."

"What made you think of that now? What does that have to do with getting our vaccinations today?" asked Jessica. "But, now that you mention it, I haven't been able to reach Rachel and Todd lately. Have you talked to them?"

"I guess it's just my female intuition, but I don't like this crowd getting vaccinated for a virus. Everybody's acting like a germ is the end of the world: it's like salmon swimming upstream—crazy. It seems an awful lot of overkill. I'm feeling very suspicious about the whole business."

"Shh. Don't let anyone hear you say that, Alice. We could get in all kinds of trouble if people narced on us for disobedience. Look what happened twenty years ago—everyone was locked in their own homes—indefinitely!"

"I'm not going to do it. Are you coming with me?"

"Yes—but where are we going?"

"Back home for now. We can decide what to do later."

The young women descended the subway stairs, not looking back lest it appear that they were looking over their shoulders, a move which would attract the attention of the Patriarchal Police or their informers. They boarded the return train, which would take them back to Sleepy Hollow.

"That wasn't so bad, was it?" a Patriarchal Policeman asked them, when they took their seats. "You can be proud that you have done your civic duty. Obedience is safety is freedom."

"Hail Patriarch," the friends replied. "Our Great Protector."

Two hours later, the commuter train pulled into the station at Sleepy Hollow, and the friends hurried to Jessica's car in the parking lot. Jessica drove Alice home, and they ordered a pizza and uncorked a bottle of wine. Her feet propped up on an ottoman, Jessica leaned back into the cushions of her chair.

"What do you make of it? Where do your suspicions take you?"

"Well, Jess, I don't trust what's in that shot. I know that it's a crime to say it, but I can't help being a skeptic, a—a rebel."

"Alice, be careful. You don't know where the listening devices are," Jessica replied in a whisper, looking nervously around her. "Obedience is safety is freedom," she said somewhat loudly, staring pointedly at her friend.

"Point taken."

The doorbell rang, and they opened it to the Patriarch Pizza delivery person.

"Hi. What happened to the usual guy—a day off?" asked Alice, when she answered the door to a girl she had never seen before.

"Dunno. Haven't seen him at work for a while. Enjoy your pizza."

Alice closed the door and turned to her friend: "It's getting dark awfully early for late summer. The sun is setting already."

When they had finished off the last slice of their pizza, Jessica picked up her keys and went to the door. The friends made plans to meet after work the next day, at a coffee shop where they would often hang out with a familiar crowd. Lying on her back on the sofa, lost in thought, Alice bade her friend a somewhat absent goodbye, and then Jessica opened the door to leave.

"Oh, God!" she screamed, "Alice! Come here!"

Alice jumped up from the sofa and hurried to her friend. By the ghostly white light of the new moon above, the Patriarch Pizza driver, crumpled and bleeding from her nose and her eyes, was illumined where she lay on the sidewalk. Alice called 911—but an ambulance had already arrived and was loading up the poor girl, even before she could finish dialing. The Patriarch Ambulance personnel were wearing strange uniforms that covered their arms and hands and even their faces, with only very small openings for their eyes. The girls closed the door and went back inside.

"Do you think it's something infectious?" asked Alice. "The way they're dressed, I mean."

"I don't know—but it's not the virus the Patriarch keeps talking about, because they say that that causes difficulty breathing, not bleeding."

"Well, those guys were sure dressed for something. How did they know before we called? And why is it so blasted dark already?"

"May I stay here with you tonight, Alice? I'm afraid to go out there right now."

Neither having slept well, both of the young women were up and about early the next morning. Together, they ventured out onto the covered porch, revisiting the scene of the night's events, their horror not diminished by the rosy light of dawn. It was a chilly morning, unusually cold for summer. But that was not what was bothering them—it was not simply the death of the pizza driver, either. Although they could not explain why, everything just *felt different*. They weren't hungry, so they shared a meagre meal of toast and black coffee, to aid themselves in coming out of their fog, after which they departed for their respective jobs. They arranged to meet for an early dinner together after work. Alice worked at the *Patriarchal News*, and everything felt weird to her that day—her co-workers were busy at their desks, as usual, but they weren't chatting it up as usual, and they seemed more focused. Jessica worked at Patriarchal Fashions, and business was really slow there—only three customers all day—ordinarily, she would tidy up the shop or read a good book when business was slow, but she could not this day, because something felt not quite right.

At the end of the workday, they rendezvoused at Patriarch Coffee for a sandwich and a latte. They talked about how quiet it had been at work all day, and they talked about their favorite television show. They kept the conversation to neutral topics because they were aware that they were being overheard. Neither friend desiring to go home alone, they lingered in the cafe until closing time. At last, Alice stood and, picking up her shoulder bag, said it was time for her to go. Jessica rose, too, and they hugged and said good-bye.

"It's dark outside—the moon is out already. Quite unreal! Is there supposed to be an eclipse? Well, I'll talk to you tomorrow, dear," she said. And then the screaming started.

The friends ran to the window. With their arms linked and their noses pressed to the glass, they searched the blackness— the dead-of-night blackness which had descended hours earlier than it should have in the summer. What they saw, by the albino rays of the too-early-risen moon, were the pallid corpses of two men and a woman heaped atop each other on the sidewalk, their blood-covered faces plainly visible in the icy illumination; the girls could also see a hysterical poodle whose leash was wound around the wrist of the slain woman. Several bystanders sheltering in the shadows beneath the awning of the café were screaming for help. Two ambulances pulled up to the sidewalk, and then the Patriarch Ambulance workers, garbed in full coveralls, began loading the casualties onto gurneys and wheeling them away. One woman, most likely the wife of one of the stricken men, was babbling deliriously. And then, suddenly, everyone became eerily quiet. As the crowd started to melt away, people hugged the buildings, instinctively feeling safer beneath the awnings, and loathe to step on the blood-soaked concrete. Jessica and Alice quietly exited the café through the rear service door—their cars were in the parking garage behind the building. After exchanging abbreviated good-nights, they got into their cars and locked their doors, but Jessica sprang forthwith out of her vehicle, knocked on her friend's window, and slid into the passenger seat of her car. By the light of the moon, she exclaimed, she had watched two people drop down dead on the sidewalk!

"I don't think we should go out there," she said. And the girls huddled in the car in the cold parking deck until sunrise.

When the sun came out, both the automobile and the pedestrian traffic increased. No one was falling to the ground. No one was screaming. The women decided to return to their homes just long enough to pack provisions for an extended trip: they would leave town for a while—at least until they understood what was happening. They would have to move quickly, before the Patriarchal Police or their observant neighbors learned what they were doing. Jessica's family owned a cabin in the Poconos, which they had not used since she was a toddler; they would go there. Once they were beyond the borders of Westchester County, they could purchase enough groceries to keep them for a week or two, and then head west.

By early afternoon, the friends had unpacked the contents of their cars and carried them into the cabin. While Alice undertook to fire up the grill to cook some veggie burgers, Jessica went for a short walk to enjoy the beautiful wood. She had not been outside for more than a few minutes before the sun set—and it was dark.

"Unbelievable!" she said out loud to herself. *Every day is shorter. This is supposed to be the Dog Days of Summer! At least the moon is nearly full—and it's bright enough to light my way back to the cabin.*

When Alice opened the door to call to Jessica that their veggie burgers were ready, she heard her friend softly say, "Oh,"—and then she watched in horror, as Jessica collapsed onto the dirt of the footpath! Both her fallen friend—and the wood beyond the doorway—were now stained a ghastly grey color by the moonlight. The moon's cursed rays glinted on the ruby-red rivulet that was streaming from Jessica's mouth and forming a halo on the ground around her head. Her body heaving with her sobs, Alice closed the door and withdrew into the bedroom. *The moon—the moon must have something to do with it—everyone I've seen die has died in the moonlight!* She pulled the blanket from the bed and wrapped herself in it, keening for her dead friend and rocking herself in her chair until dawn.

Once the moon had set, Alice secreted the cars among the trees, lest they be discovered by the Patriarchal Police, and then she searched for a shovel. When she found one in the lean-to shed, she dragged her friend's body into a thicket and buried her in the woods. She found a hammer and nails in the shed, too, and with them she began to cover the windows to protect herself from the lethal light of the mone.

The Patriarch

"**Y**our Eminence, may I clarify your most generous proposal —in exchange for serving you, I will be given dominion over the earth?" The Patriarch looked beatific, and an otherworldly smile spread over all his features, as he contemplated the benefits of such a prospect.

"Of course. You do realize that I require unstinting obedience."

"Undoubtedly, Your Eminence," the Patriarch said, his left eye glowing green. "I wish to emphasize that I am aware of the great honor you do me."

"Then there should be no difficulty in fulfilling our mission." The Patriarch's right eye emitted a green glow, "Now, let us get down to this business of the vaccinations."

"Eminence," answered the Patriarch, "Our propaganda campaign has, thus far, succeeded beyond expectations. People are flocking to the vaccination sites." Green smoke trailed into his left nostril from his right nostril.

"Patriarch," he answered himself, exhaling green smoke. "We will discuss the moonlight at our next meeting."

"Farewell, Your Eminence," the Patriarch, replied, bowing, as the green vapors from his ears and nostrils wafted away, and the air began to clear.

Jason's breath caught, as he strove to take it all in: "vaccination,"

"moonlight." And what was all that green vapor? He was observing the Patriarch from a weird angle, secreted, as he was, in the air duct above the Patriarch's desk. Was the Patriarch mad? The way he was talking to himself—maybe he was just rehearsing a planned conversation.

He eased himself through the ductwork, crawling backward toward the utility door in the ceiling. He glanced quickly at the grating. No, the Patriarch did not appear to have heard him: he seemed, rather, to be in a daze. Jason reached the trap door in the ceiling, and he put his ear to it—no sounds from the hallway below. He slid the door and jumped through the opening into the hall, and he pulled the string to replace the door.

Sidling along the walls, he moved toward the Patriarch's suite, and he saw a green light emanating from beneath the door. He hurried to the stairwell and ran down the stairs to the first floor, and then he exited the building. It was only three o'clock, and it was July, but the sun was setting, and he had to get home quickly.

Home was in Sleepy Hollow. He boarded the train, careful to avoid eye contact with the other passengers, or with the crew—there were few enough of them, these days—and he huddled in his seat, training his eyes upon the swiftly moving scenery, watching the sun move closer to the horizon. When he reached his stop, he raced to his car and peeled out of the parking lot. He entered his house only moments before the sun dipped below the horizon.

"I was worried," his wife said. "I was afraid you would be out after dark."

"I made it, Joan," he said, as he made the rounds of the windows, making sure they were secured against the night.

"Did you find out anything?" she asked.

"The Patriarch talks to himself, and there is a green vapor that glows in his office. I think he was smoking something."

"What about the vaccine? What about the moonlight?"

"All he said to himself was that the vaccinations were progressing. And he said he'd get back to himself about the moonlight."

"What if he wasn't talking to himself?"

"Joan, there was no one else there. He was just standing alone, and the green vapor kept coming out of his nose and mouth. If there was anyone else in the room, I couldn't see or hear him."

"How long do you think we can get away with not getting the vaccine?" she asked her husband. "They'll catch on to us sooner or later. They'll check our story, I'm sure."

"Honestly, I think we'd better plan on leaving the city soon. Let's take that trip to the Poconos that we've been wanting to take. Let's make it an extended vacation. I don't like being in the city now—people dying every night—only at night, and the Patriarch's obsession with forcing everyone to get this injection. It doesn't add up in my book, and my instincts are shouting to me to run while we can."

"We'd better go tonight—in case anyone observed your activities at Headquarters today—we don't want to add the Patriarchal Police to our problems."

"By the looks of the sky, a storm is coming. Let's get packing."

The days were fast becoming shorter, with less than six hours of daylight. It was always cold now, and Alice, running low on food in her cabin in the woods, one afternoon drove to the nearest town. In the little store there, she bought the entirety of the foodstuffs that remained on the shelves, as well as much fresh food as she could eat before it went bad. The owner of the store told her that she would be closing that day, as the town had pretty much emptied out—most everyone had died suddenly during the night, bleeding out, or they had moved away. She answered "No," when Alice asked her whether she were going to leave, too; the woman said that she wouldn't know where to go, it being only herself and her invalid husband. They were going to try to wait it out, whatever it was, at home.

"Only it's so cold now and dark most of the time. We don't know what to make of it."

Alice wished her well and set out for her hideout in the woods. There were no other cars on the two-lane country road. She had not spoken to anyone in a month—fearing discovery by the Patriarchal Police—and she had not so much as made a phone call in all that time. Now she was considering the words of the shopkeeper. *So, people were still dying, and others had fled. To where? Why could no one explain the waning sunlight and the rash of deaths? Why was the Patriarch not doing something?*

Her attention was arrested by ominous points of light in the violet twilight firmament. She looked at the clock on her dashboard—1:30 P.M. The dusky radiance of the evening had already succeeded the robin's egg blue of the day, a transition she had failed to notice while she had been turning the woman's words over in her mind. Bright dots of white light sparkled in the sky—brighter than Venus or Polaris—and they *moved*! What's more—they were circling the moon! She turned off her head-lights and pulled into her long driveway, parked her car among the trees, where it would be difficult to spot, and then carried her groceries inside.

It was dark by the time she had brought everything in. She had just closed the refrigerator door, when the cabin began to shake, causing her to lose her balance and tumble to the pinewood floor. She gripped the counter to pull herself up and then went into the sitting room, where she sat upon the couch, afraid that the ceiling was going to fall on her head. She made her way to the window, still holding onto the furniture, for the floor continued to shake beneath her feet. In the black of night, she could see only a green light . . . flickering through the trees in the distance.

They were driving over the suspension bridge, the dark city now visible in their rear-view mirror, when Jason shouted:

"Look!"

He guided his car to the narrow outside lane, shifted the gear into park and craned his neck to look out the back window. The Headquarters was aglow with a green light!

"What is that?" his wife asked.

"I don't know—but we're getting out of here."

They drove into the stygian night, frightened, because the night was when people tended to die, often be found the next day, usually after they had bled to death. The sky before them was overcast, moon and stars hidden behind an opaque pall of dark clouds; and when they had left the city behind, a storm broke, loosing torrents of water upon their windshield. To avoid hydroplaning in the standing water, Jason drove in the middle of the road, for there were no other vehicles out that night. When the downpour ended and the clouds started to drift slowly away, the stars started to twinkle merrily.

Joan said, "Shooting stars! They're supposed to be good omens."

Watching the stars, though, they became troubled. The stars were not falling in the usual manner of shooting stars, but were moving in circles—around the moon! The moon had come out of hiding, too, now that the clouds had departed.

Joan clutched her abdomen and groaned. Jason turned. "What's the matter? Are you all right?"

"Oh, it hurts! Oh, Jason. What's happening to me?"

He pulled into a parking lot, stopped the car, and enfolded his wife in his arms. She began to scream, and he held her tighter, with tears running down his face.

"Honey, what is it? What can I do to help you?"

For answer, she whimpered and sobbed. Then, thick blood began to darken her cotton skirt—it soaked the car seat and ran down her legs. Jason held his wife tighter and prayed, weeping, sure that she was dying before his eyes. She became still. He held his breath. And then, a moment later, he opened his eyes. She was breathing—faintly. And between her legs was a small mound of flesh, a baby they had not known she was carrying, it having lived only a short time in her womb. He cried for his baby, and for Joan; and he cried all the more for joy that she was still alive! He eased his wife from his arms, and then he got out of the car. He opened the hatch in the back, yanked a small suitcase roughly out of it, set it on the ground and opened the clasps. Removing a towel, he wrapped his dead child in it. Then he undressed his unconscious wife, cleaned her with another towel, and covered her with a nightgown. The darkness was unrelieved now by any celestial light, for the clouds had again blanketed the sky, but the interior lights of the car were sufficient for his sorrowful work. When Joan began to stir, he kissed her face softly; when she was awake, he gave her water to moisten her mouth. They resumed their journey, as dawn began to redden the horizon.

"I see. The women have always been synchronized with the moon. They are lunar creatures, whether one recognizes this fact or not. Brilliant, Excellency! Brilliant!" The green vapor entered the Patriarch's left ear, and his left eye glowed green. And then his right eyes glowed with the emerald light. The vapor was emitted by his mouth as he spoke, and it hovered there, when he said, "Patriarch, you do understand, I see. Which is why you have been selected to assist us in the implementation of Project Diana." From the mouth of the Patriarch, whose eyes both glowed with an emerald luster, a jade mist churned about his head.

"It is an honor, Your Eminence, to serve you in all ways," responded the Patriarch. "May I inquire when I might have the happiness of beholding Your Eminence as you are, Great Lord, to see your august form, as opposed to hearing you in my brain—which is a superlative pleasure, indeed?"

Again, from his own mouth, as the green mist swirled with great energy about him: "When Project Diana is accomplished."

"Ah, yes. The women. Undoubtedly, Excellency. I shall see that your will is expedited," the Patriarch replied, as the mist dissipated from the room.

He picked up the phone: "By Patriarchal Proclamation, twice the usual number shall receive the vaccination tomorrow. The usual serums for the males and for the females are to be implemented. Barricade the city, that none may leave, until further directives have been issued."

He directed his secretary to call his chauffer, and he would have skipped to the elevator, were not the adoption of such an indecorous gait unbecoming to the current Patriarch of the land—and the future Absolute Ruler of the Earth.

Women's Fertility Studies Division

"Dr. Randall, what do you think is the ultimate end of Project Diana? I mean, just why are we making this serum?"

"Dr. Stokes, please consider what you are saying, and who might be listening. Is it not enough to know that you are doing your duty to the Patriarchy?"

"Cool down, Doctor. You know that curiosity is a necessary trait in a scientist. A better understanding of just how our work fits into the greater aspects of Project Diana might lead to further breakthroughs."

"Dr. Stokes. You realize that you are approaching forbidden territory, and I refuse to discuss this anymore with you. I shall expect your data on the alterations in human male DNA in response to the serum."

"Roger, righto, Doctor. Back to work, then."

A thousand pairs of green eyes were fixed upon the speaker, although an observer would not have known that those eyes were green, because the thousand faces behind the eyes were swathed in black cloth, tiny slits the only difference between blindness and sightedness for all those people. If an observer got very close, he still could not have seen their eyes, for those gathered in the auditorium in the great observatory were wearing dark glasses over their cloth-covered faces.

When the black-garbed figure on the dais at the front of the auditorium knelt down before the far-space surveillance telescope, the thousand green-eyed devotees followed suit. His back to them, the priest raised his arms, and the congregation prostrated themselves upon the floor.

"Goddess. Mother. Source of Life. And Source of Death. Creator of Life. Bringer of Destruction. Huntress of Men. Raise us up, your servants. For love of You. For fear of You. To honor Your Holy Power. We offer this Sacrifice."

The priest remained in that position as two men wrapped in black led forth a third man, likewise cloaked. The priest bowed down, covering his face with his gloved palms, and the congregation covered their faces, too. The skylight above opened, bathing the dark auditorium in chalky, poisonous moonlight; and the two men who had brought the third forward pulled off the prisoner's robes, allowing the celestial light to shine upon his naked body. Screaming, the man turned to run from the light, but before he was able to take a single step into the darkness, his legs gave way, and he fell to the floor. His life-blood gushed out from his orifices, a steadily widening circle of red upon the white marble. When he heard the sound of the skylight closing, the priest rose; and, turning to face the people, he said,

"The Goddess is well-pleased. Return to your homes."

The priest, with his acolytes, went to the bloodless man. Two robed men lifted the carcass and carried it away. Two more, with little shovels and syphons, retrieved the elixir of life from the marble, while it was still liquid enough to harvest.

"Hang On!" Jason shouted, turning the wheel sharply to the left, trying to keep their car from plummeting over the edge of the mountain, as the pulsating of the earth caused the road to move beneath them. Joan—her fingers white with the effort—clung to the dashboard and the door handle to keep herself from flying all over the car, and to keep the door from being flung open. "There's an exit sign—I'm getting us off this road—just hold tight!"

With great effort, Jason maintained his grip on the steering wheel and kept the bouncing car on the pavement. He guided it toward the exit sign, followed the ramp to its termination at an unmowed meadow, and then drove the car into the tall grass. Placing the gear in park, he turned to look at Joan. She was staring out the window, wordless and pale beneath her opaque covering. Jason took her face into both his hands and turned it toward him. He kissed her, over and over, her forehead, her lips, her cheeks, kissed her through the black gabardine, murmuring, "It's okay, it's okay." She screamed wildly and then she broke down, sobbing—and Jason held her in his arms until her tears ceased.

Thirty minutes later, when the earth had stopped its trembling, Joan, in a nonchalant voice, advised that they seek shelter. Jason wholeheartedly agreed—for they were both drained. He followed the road signs to a national park, where there would be camping sites and cabins not visible from the main road.

"When was the last time you saw the sun?" Joan asked, as they pulled into the park entrance, and Jason replied that it must have been the day before last, just before they left home. "More than forty-eight hours without daylight," she responded, her voice trailing away.

"One thing we'll have plenty of—firewood," Jason replied, forcing himself to be upbeat. "These cabins in the woods usually cost and arm and a leg, but tonight we'll get one for free." He drove their car into a campground, offering her choice of cabin. Joan chose a small one on the far end of the row of log structures, and they pulled up to the porch. Jason forced the lock with a screwdriver, and they entered the pretty sitting room.

"Let's bring in what we'll need tonight, and then I'll hide the car in the woods," he said.

After they had brought food and a change of clothing inside, Jason secreted the car within a grove of trees, and Joan covered the windows with blankets she found in the closet. When Jason returned, they checked their cell phones—they were dead—and, although there was electricity, the television was out of order, too. Standing before the cold fireplace in the rustic room, they clung tightly to each other, saying nothing, each pressing his face into the other's shoulder, so that they could feel the warmth of each other's breath. Words were not adequate for their grief and terror.

Sighing, Jason opened his eyes, let go of his wife—sprang back. A green light was shining through the keyhole of the door! He extracted his sunglasses from his shirt pocket, put them over his eyes, and went to the window. Feeling his face, to ascertain that his skin was veiled—all but his eyes—by his ebony moonlight mask, he turned back just a tiny corner of the blanket which was covering the window—and he peered into the darkness. A neon green light was emanating from the forest—the same emerald glow which they had seen when they had driven out from the city. Pulling his head back from the window, he replaced the blanket, securing it carefully to block the toxic rays.

"I'm going to find out where that green light is coming from," he said.

"No, Jason. Don't go!" she cried, "Don't leave me!"

"I won't stay long, Joan. Honey, we need to know what's out there," he replied, saddened by the thought of leaving her—and frightened of what he might discover out there. "If we're not alone, we need to know it, and then we'll know what we should do."

"If you go, I'm going, too."

They fastened each other's protective covering, making certain that not even a square centimeter of their bodies was revealed. When they were ready, they pulled on their gloves and placed dark glasses over the slits which they had cut in the fabric for their eyes, taking every precaution to avoid exposure to the deadly light. They crept along the side of the cabin, keeping out of the moonlight—and then they sprinted across the yard to the cover provided by the foliage, almost tripping over their long black robes. Concealed within a group of large bushes, they trained their flashlights on the mossy floor of the forest, and then they carefully picked their steps as they crept among the roots and branches, toward the green light.

As they drew nearer to the light, they felt the earth vibrating. Each held the other's hand, squeezing so tightly that it hurt, but they dared not speak. Hugging the wide trunks of the enormous, old-growth trees which provided them cover, they continued their progress toward the green luminosity. Joan sensed rather than heard her husband catch his breath, and she halted. Jason knelt to the ground, pulling Joan down with him. She twisted her neck to see what it was that he had seen—moving green forms, ill-defined, yet discreet—a strange kind of glimmering beings. Stealthily, they slunk away from the creatures, ever so slowly, aware that the crackling of a single twig could spell their deaths.

When they reached their cabin, they ran past it—bolted into the woods on the other side of it, fleeing the hideous creatures. As they moved among the trees, blind in the unrelieved darkness of the forest, they collided with a soft form—a creature of some kind—it emitted a stifled moan. It was a person—a person swaddled like themselves in black cloth! The person felt through the layers of fabric for their hands, and finding them, guided the couple away from the luminous creatures, further into the wood.

Seated before the fireplace in her cabin, Alice and her guests exchanged their stories—how they had fled the city, afraid of the vaccine; of all the sudden deaths by bleeding; the disappearances of so many people they knew.

"Oh, and the Patriarch Ambulance drivers—that hazmat gear they were wearing—something was up."

"It may have been just protection from the moonlight—"

"But they were wearing it in the daylight!"

"And what's with all the people dying when the moon is out?"

"I know that somehow it's related to the vaccine. Let me tell you what I saw in the air duct at Headquarters—"

Eventually, their conversation came around to Joan's miscarriage.

"Oh, my dearest one, how horrible. I am so sorry," Alice said, as Joan held a wad of black gabardine to her eyes. "I lost my best friend, and you your baby." After a few moments of silent commiseration, she added, "You know, I haven't had a menstrual cycle for months—not since the days started growing shorter—not since people started dying. I've been thinking it was a hormonal response to my fear and anxiety, but maybe it is more than that."

Jason responded, "Come to think of it, Jack's wife lost their baby last week. You know Jack, honey—I work with him." Joan nodded her head.

Alice told them of the old couple—they had died the day after they had been vaccinated. She had found them with their eyes open—and they both had green eyes.

"Everyone in the city seems to have green eyes, now that you mention it. I was remarking on that fact to Jack my last day at work. We were talking about it because Jack was telling me that his eyes had changed color—they were brown before."

"Did Jack get the vaccine?"

"Yes, he did. A couple of days before we left town."

"Has everyone had enough to eat? I'll start cleaning up, while you relax. It is so nice to have company. In a little while, we can put our heads together and maybe make some kind of plans for tomorrow— What's that noise? My God!"

"Quick! Pack everything you can carry. We'll make one run to the car! We've got to get out of here. That's a helicopter! I'll get a bag of food."

"Joan, here's a bag, you get some food, too."

"Alice, where's your car? Everyone ready? Check your moonbeam covers! Your gloves—and sunglasses, too! Let's go!"

"Joan, Jason! This way!" Alice said, as she led the way to her

car. She ran as fast as she could in her flowing robes, not stopping until she reached the car, when she heard

"Joan! Joan! Oh, God, no! Joan!"

Alice dropped her bag of food and slowly made her way back toward the cabin. She fell to her knees and vomited her dinner on the ground—Joan was being carried away by four iridescent green figures, grotesque beings with indefinite, amorphous lines, but beings nonetheless. They were carrying a seemingly lifeless Joan into the trees. Alice took hold of herself and cautiously moved toward Jason, who was lying prone in the dirt path.

"Dr. Randall, it is a privilege to have you in our laboratory," gushed Dr. Warren, beside himself at being in the presence of the great man. "I would be honored to give you a tour of our Women's Fertility Studies Division, of which, as you know, I am the administrator."

"Dr. Warren, we have a full day of meetings planned. Why don't we walk quickly through Women's en route to the board room? As we walk, you can update me on your progress."

"An honor, Dr. Randall, an honor. If it pleases you, follow me in this direction," Dr. Warren answered, gesturing, as he spoke, toward the elevator which led down to the sub-basements of the Patriarchal Center for Health Advancement.

Four stories down they went, as Dr. Warren enumerated his achievements in the study of Female Fertility, especially in relation to lunar cycles. When the doors of the elevator parted, the men stepped forward toward another door. Dr. Warren flashed his electronic badge, and the door slid open. As they entered the brightly-lit, white-tiled room, two men, clad in lab coats, pushed a gurney past them, on which an unconscious woman lay, covered to her neck by a sheet. The woman stirred, and then she opened her eyes. As she opened her mouth to scream, an officious attendant placed a cloth soaked in chloroform over her face, and Joan fell once more into a swoon.

The Dianic Priesthood

"I'm not kidding! Their eyes are blue!"

"I've had enough of those freaks. They're putting us all at risk. The Patriarch says we need one hundred percent compliance with the vaccine!"

"Who the hell do they think they are!"

The four green-eyed men rose from their red vinyl seats in a corner booth in the Patriarch Pub. George quaffed the remaining quarter of his draft beer, set the glass down hard on the Formica-covered table, and followed Mike, Ron, and Ed to the door. The men removed their garments from the coat hooks and helped each other into their moonlight-protective cloaks, and then donned their gloves and dark glasses. They left the pub together.

"May I help you gentlemen?" the green-eyed librarian asked the men, as they swept past the circulation desk and headed straight for the reading room. She lowered her eyes to the desk and rifled through a sheaf of papers on it. When she heard the sounds of furniture breaking and books falling from the shelves, she retreated into her office. Fifteen minutes later, she resumed her position at the front desk, just in time to see two Patriarch Ambulance drivers pushing a gurney covered by a blood-soaked sheet out the glass front doors.

Theodore, on his way to meet his cousin Marty at the library, observed the ambulance drivers loading their vehicle. Instead of entering the library, he kept on walking, betraying no interest in the activity on the street. He walked past his automobile. Three blocks later, he turned into a tight alley, turned again at the street at the end of the alley, and doubled back to his car. When he saw that there were no people on the street, he got into the driver's seat and pulled his car onto the road. First, he drove five miles toward the freeway, which he entered, heading south; two exits from that, he left the freeway and then got back onto it, driving north this time. From there, he went home. He parked his car in the garage of a vacant house a block away from his own bungalow, and he walked through the backyards as he made his way home.

"Teddy, I'm so glad you're back. I was worried," Sandra said, as she hurried to the door. Through the voluminous opaque fabric he was wearing, she hugged him tight and said, "How is Marty?"

Theodore pushed her away and dropped down onto the sofa; he put his head in his hands and began to cry. Sandra flew to his side and joined him on the sofa. Blowing his nose, Theodore told her what had happened.

"You know we have to leave," she said, as she donned her coat and her moonlight-blocking cloak and hood. She left to bring the car back to their house. When she returned, the couple placed their suitcases in the car—they had already been packed, in anticipation of such a contingency. "I wish we could call Maggie. I wish the phones were working."

Maggie was cold and hungry. She had resorted to rationing her food. She knew she was fortunate to possess three cases of tuna and several boxes of crackers, but in the last month, she had not been able to uncover any more food: she had been to all the stores and houses within ten miles, but they had all been cleared out before she got to them. She was sick with worry for her sister Sandra and for her brother-in-law, who had remained in the city; and she resolved to check on them while she was driving around in search of a passed-over cache of supplies. There must be something useful in one of the small towns which were scattered between the A-frame house in the forest—the basement of which she had been calling home for the last four months—and her sister's home in town.

It was only last summer when she had come upon the one-time owners of the house lying dead in their front yard, their decaying bodies ringed in blood, desiccated by time to the consistency of dried paint. From the dead man's pocket, she had removed his keys, and she had foraged through the house for provisions. In the garage, she had discovered many filled gasoline cans; and after she had dragged the bodies into the shrubbery, she had secreted the car and the gas cans in the surrounding forest. And then she had moved into the basement, carrying all the stores of the kitchen and the pantry down the steps. Now, though, her supplies were running low, and she had already scavenged every house and business in the vicinity.

When Maggie arrived in town, she left her car behind a vacant house two blocks from her sister's home, and—staying close to the houses and darting from bush to bush in order to avoid the open spaces where she would be seen more easily—she slipped through the neighbors' backyards. She was nervous. Since summer, she had not ventured so far from her warren in the woods. It was last summer when the rash of unexplained deaths from bleeding and the disappearance of the sun had sent her into hiding. The Patriarch had vowed to protect everyone, and he had even come up with a vaccine—overnight, apparently—that would keep them all safe. It did not add up for Maggie. Why were people dying when the moon was out—and how could a vaccine prevent that? No one had answered her questions. Many would only look at her with suspicion in their eyes when she asked. Some people had seemed nervous that she had even questioned the directives of the Patriarch. Some of her friends died, and some disappeared. Maggie fled.

The street was silent, most—perhaps, all—of the houses seemingly unoccupied. In every yard the grass was overgrown, and heaps of refuse were piled around overflowing trash cans. Hearing the sounds of activity as she approached her sister's house, Maggie dropped quickly to her hands and knees; and she crept low through the hedgerows until she could see Sarah's driveway—and then she had to hold her mouth closed with both of her hands to stop herself from crying out.

A Patriarch Ambulance was there—in Sarah's driveway—and a person covered by a head-to-toe moonlight-protective suit was fastening the double doors in the back of the ambulance. Another person, likewise garbed, was using a pipette to siphon blood from the driveway—and he was putting the salvaged blood into a biological materials container. Stifling her tears, Maggie retreated, creeping backwards awkwardly, on her hands and knees through the gardens and flowerbeds behind the houses. When she reached her car, she had to resist the desire to fall to pieces, to be hysterical. Setting her face like stone, she drove her car over the lawn and then onto the street.

As she drove, Maggie could not help but stare—through the small openings in her hood and through the dark glasses which she wore over them—at the moving points of light in the sky. The glowing, silvery spots were, as usual, ringing the malicious white orb in the black ever-after night. The noxious, chalk-light of the moon was reiterated by the grey clouds surrounding the Huntress, Diana, much as a billowing court train adorns an empress.

"Bring me up to date on the blood situation. Have the priests been satisfied?" The Patriarch demanded of Dr. Randall. He had no need to open his mouth to make himself understood; neither had Dr. Randall to move his lips when he ventured his reply. As a matter of fact, the bottle-green fog which was swirling into and out of the various orifices of their bodies efficiently executed the offices of communication between the two men—and between the men and their cosmic overlords, as well. His green eyes ablaze with a spinach-green fluorescence, Dr. Randall responded as he exhaled the tinted fumes,

"The Priesthood of Diana has successfully concluded their Sacrifice of the Full Moon, and they continue their work to amass stores of the Elixir of Life. What *do* the priests need the blood for, Patriarch?"

"Need I remind you, Doctor, that your business is limited to Health Advancement? I hope that I will never have to mention that again."

"Pardon, Patriarch. You are quite right."

"What is the progress in Hematology?"

"We are making substantial headway in the development of a serum which disposes human blood to hemorrhage when the gravitational pull of the moon exerts its influence upon the human organism. Further work is needed in the development of mechanisms to control the processes. Our investigative teams in the Patriarch Ambulances continue to gather data in the field, complementing the research conducted in our labs."

"Provide an update in Female Fertility, if you please."

"Vivisection has revealed numerous ways in which the human female responds to the lunar cycle. Our team is working to extrapolate practical applications from the data. Furthermore, we are investigating the differences between hormonal responses in women who have received the vaccine, women who have not been administered the serum, and women who have been given a placebo. Some of the work has been conducted here, in the Patriarchal Center for Health Advancement; additional work has been conducted on board Dianic vessels, beyond the power of gravity." An olive-green mist escaped from his nostrils, as he concluded his remarks.

"Seismology is correlating tidal and plate tectonic data relative to lunar influence, and the involvement of the human female in these processes."

The room filled with the jade-colored vapor which streamed from the ears and eyes of the Patriarch, some of which the Great Man blew from his mouth as if he were smoking a pipe. The miasma drifted around the imposing mahogany desk, slid along the priceless Asiatic carpet, wafted through the air vent, and seeped out around the door frame. When the mist had dissipated, the Patriarch and Dr. Randall regarded each other, blinking to clear their vision.

"We are pleased that Project Diana is proceeding on schedule. Keep up the good work, Doctor," the Patriarch spoke, his words resulting from the combined efforts of his lips, tongue, and larynx this time.

"It was a pleasure to see you, again, Your Eminence. I am honored to be of service," replied the doctor, bowing to the Patriarch and wondering why his head felt so strange.

"Blessings of the Goddess, Brother," replied the black-hooded vicar of Diana, looking down upon the priest. "Has Science delivered the Elixir of Life as promised?"

"Yes, Master. The life-blood extracted from the subjects in Fertility has greatly enriched our sacrifice. May our offering gratify the Goddess and Her Most Noble Messengers."

"Who has been selected to place the gifts upon the altar?"

"I, Master."

"Array yourself for the ceremony," the High Priest ordered the kneeling brother, who was covered in a black shroud, as were all of the priests of The Huntress.

Two ebony-robed figures came into the room and lifted the priest to his feet; and then they led him into an antechamber, where they exchanged his dress for folds of white silk and a white silken cowl to cover his head, and they placed white gloves upon his hands. When the priests returned their white brother and resumed their stations before the High Priest, three more dark figures entered the compartment, each one bearing a gold vessel which was brimming with a thick, crimson fluid. When each had placed his vessel upon a golden tray on a marble table, the white-robed priest lifted the tray, and the entire party proceeded to the door—two black figures before the white priest, and three behind him, with the High Priest at the rear. All donned their protective glasses over the hoods which shielded their faces, and then the great doors of hammered silver swung open. The priestly entourage walked into a moon-bathed courtyard, where the High Priest offered a prayer to Diana. After the ritual was concluded, all turned to re-enter the Pavilion of the Huntress—all except the white priest, who was still bearing the golden tray with the gold cups filled with rich, warm gore. When the double doors closed behind the black priests, the white priest shivered, partly because it was always so cold now that the sun had fled, and partly because he was afraid.

He remained still, reverently bearing the sacred burden but, when he felt the earth begin to tremble, instinctively, he raised his face to the stygian heavens. Though his eye-slits were covered by dark glasses, he was able to discern several moving points of bright light in the raven blackness—one of which seemed to be plunging straight toward the place where he was standing. Afraid of the wrath of the Goddess—and afraid of the wrath of the priests should he retreat to the Pavilion of the Huntress—he remained where he was standing. A humming sound, to which he, at first, had scarcely attended, was becoming louder, more insistent in its volume and pitch so that he must heed it. It became manifest to him that the white spot of light which had, initially, only *seemed* to be moving in his direction was most assuredly following a trajectory into the courtyard.

With a thud, the silver metal vessel landed the in frost-covered field, and the earth shuddered in reply. The white-robed priest felt an icy coldness in his veins—a coldness which could not be measured in Fahrenheit, Celsius, or Kelvin, but which was as quantifiable as eternity and endless as damnation. An aperture appeared in the silver ship, unaccompanied by any of the sounds which typically accompany the opening of doors and windows. From it, a glowing green form emerged, nebulous, and then another, and then another, and then more. The imprecise green blurs which emerged began to assume more definite forms—silvery green creatures who stood upon two human feet and had the heads of hounds and falcons' wings. The white priest held his ground and lifted the offering before him, even as the shimmering alien hunters advanced. He did not scream—not until they had pierced his veins and his arteries and began to drink therefrom. The priest fell to the frozen grass before the tray hit the gore-covered ground. The blood-drinkers dissolved into formless green clouds and wafted back to their vessel, shimmering, infinite hues of green.

Extinction

"Triumphant Goddess,
Vanquisher of all other gods,
Huntress who has slain the very sun.
Divine Lady who has sent Messengers from the sky,
She who hunts in perpetual night,
Diana, we adore thee.
With our blood, we quench thy thirst,
With our life blood, we honor thee,
Darkness and beauty, all the endless night of our lives."

The High Priest turned from the far-space surveillance telescope to face the congregation. "The Goddess has come lightly to the earth, gliding on a silvery moonbeam. Her royal chalices of silver bear Her Divine Messengers from the firmament unto our insignificant orb. Verily, Lady Diana hath crushed the forgotten idols of our benighted race. Else ye die, do homage and obedience unto Our Lady."

The thousand disciples knelt upon the floor, a charcoal-colored sea rippling in the great hall of the Observatory.

Maggie pushed the gas pedal down hard, driving fast, away from the city, stopping at her house only long enough to fill her van with her remaining stores of food and water, blankets, and gasoline. When she had done, she climbed into the driver's seat. Her heart, caught up in a paroxysm of palpitations, was executing sickening somersaults, for she had, over the last few months, enjoyed a small sense of security in her cellar hideout, but it was no longer safe. With both hands, she gripped the steering wheel tightly, willing herself to inhale deeply, both to slow her heart and to steady her nerve.

She headed west, deep into the mountains, where the freeways exits were spaced farther apart, where the raging rivers of billboards dwindled to a trickle, and where truck stops were few and far between—and where there would be more places to hide. She had been driving for hours, ever since morning, when she left home to go into the city. So when the signposts on the side of the road announced the entrance to the national park, she decided to spend the night there. When she reached the camping area, she drove her car over the hoary, frosted grass and parked it behind the central cabin in a row of box-shaped log structures. There was no sign of people—no lights in the darkness except for the lethal light of the moon, and the ever-circulating bright points of white light that danced demonically about the spiteful crescent—which appeared to her as a devil's horn on this frigid night.

She did not know what to do now, for she was tired, unable to think past finding a place to hide and to sleep. Perhaps she would be able to think when she had slept. She locked the car and walked toward the front of the cabin, patting the black baize on her face to wipe the tears before they froze on her cold cheeks. She crept cautiously among the shadows of the cabin wall, first inspecting the lay of her cloak and her gloves and hood to make sure she was completely covered, and then ascertaining that her glasses were on properly—necessary precautions to avoid the exposure of her flesh to the celestial poison. To avoid detection, she did not utilize her flashlight; thus, only the toxic light illumined her path. She slunk around the corner to the front porch, dropping to her hands and knees when she neared the door—to avoid a patch of moonlight—and reached up to try the doorknob.

Jason said, "The green light. The spaceship-thing—it had a green light—just like I saw in the Patriarch's office. The same swirling green colors that the Patriarch was breathing in and out, and which was going in and out of his ears and eyes, too—when he was talking to himself—"

"Maybe he wasn't talking to himself," interjected Alice, "Maybe he was talking to the green light or smoke or whatever it was. Maybe *it* was talking to *him*!"

"*Shhh*—I hear something," Jason whispered, pulling Alice to him. "There's something at the door." He pulled Alice back, drawing her into the bedroom as the front door was slowly opened, allowing the noxious beams to enter the room. Crouching on the hardwood floor behind the bedroom door, Jason checked his hood and felt for his dark glasses, and then he peeked around the door: a form enveloped in black fabric was crawling through the doorway. Jason watched the thing close the door behind itself. He called out,

"Who are you? What do you want?"

Maggie began to back away—and Jason called again, "Who are you? Why are you here?"

"I just wanted a place to sleep," Maggie answered him.

"Who are you? How many are with you?" asked Jason.

"It's only me. I'm alone. I can leave if you don't want me here."

"Let her stay," whispered Alice. She and Jason emerged from the bedroom and went to Maggie. After Alice packed some rags into the crevices to choke the deadly beams which were seeping around the door, the three fugitives shared a bottle of orange juice and a can of beans before the fireplace, and then they exchanged their stories.

When Maggie reached the portion of her narrative in which the ambulance driver had siphoned the blood from her sister's driveway, Jason spat in disgust and said, "They make me sick! They're ghouls! Vampires!"

"That's it!" exclaimed Alice. "They live only in the dark. They cause people to bleed to death. They collect the blood. They really are vampires."

"You might be on to something," responded Jason, tapping the floor with his glass. "What about the spaceships—are they vampires from space?"

"As crazy as it sounds, that might be what they are," Maggie said thoughtfully. "How on earth could the Patriarch save us from vampires with a vaccine, though?"

"The vaccine is most likely not designed to save *us*. The Patriarch is creepy." Jason told Maggie what he had seen when he watched the Patriarch from his perch in the ductwork above his office. "Since I'm probably going to die, anyway, I want to get to the bottom of this. I am going to do a little more snooping. I want to know who plans to dispatch me, and why!"

"How are you going to do that?" asked Alice.

"I think I'll go right to the source—the Patriarchal Center for Health Advancement. Isn't that where they do all their research and make the vaccine and stuff?"

"Do you think they'll just allow you to come in? And then politely answer your questions?"

"I'll find a way to get in—just like I found a way to spy on the Patriarch."

"I'll go with you," Alice and Maggie said at the same time.

Maggie being so tired, they decided to sleep for a few hours first and then drive to the Center when they were rested.

Amy, Midge, and Joan had been sharing the same cell in Female Fertility for some weeks now. They had been poked and prodded, injected, and subjected to electrical shocks. Their urine, blood, saliva, and vaginal secretions had been studied, and their skin cells removed for microscopic study. They despaired of ever seeing the outside again, and they were afraid life had pretty much ceased in the cold darkness beyond the walls of their prison—the eternal darkness which would eventually lead to the extermination of all animal and plant life on the earth. From the comments of their keepers, they assumed they had each been artificially inseminated while they were sedated.

"Vivisection!" whispered Amy. "I heard the attendant use that word as the group walked by our cell. Do they mean us?" Her eyes were wide as she breathed her words into the ears of her fellow research subjects.

"They sicken me, those monsters—those bloody vampires!" said Midge, and she spat on the floor. "Blood, blood everywhere and not a drop to drink."

"Do you think they could be—actual vampires? I mean, what's with all the bleeding deaths and all the bottling up of the dead people's blood?" Joan ventured. "What if this place is a blood bank of sorts?"

"If blood is really what they're after, then this place is an agricultural research center—and we are the agriculture," said Midge through clenched teeth. "I'd like to slit the throats of those scientists and test their blood."

"Honey, if they're talking vivisection, we may just have to do that. I'd rather die fighting a vampire than end up on the dissecting table," Amy said quietly, with an unwavering voice.

They made a plan: whoever was taken the next time would put up a fight, and the other two would jump on the attendant and take his keys. The three captives retired to their pallets on the cold, hard floor and shivered under the scraps of fabric which served for their blankets. It was not long before they heard the tinkling of an attendant's keyring, and when they heard a key turning the tumblers in the lock, they put their plan into play.

"It's your turn, my little beauty, although I can't say how long you will continue to be beautiful." Chuckling as he opened the door, the lab assistant entered the cell and then reached down to pull Amy to her feet. "You bitch!" he cried, for she had bitten his hand and torn the flesh from his knuckles with her teeth. He struck her face with his good hand, and Amy dug her nails into his calf. Launching profanities at her, the man seized her by her hair, and then Joan and Midge rushed him, knocking him off his feet. He let go of Amy's hair as he fell, and Joan seized the keys from his belt loop. While he was engaged in employing his good fist to subdue the other women, Joan plunged a key into his eye. The women bolted from the cell, leaving their jailer rolling on the floor, roaring in pain.

"We can't just walk out the front door," Midge said.

"Can we find an air duct?" asked Joan. "My husband was able to sneak around the Headquarters by crawling through the ventilation system. Do you think we can get out that way?"

"Unless we see a better way, I think we should give it a try. If we can get inside the ductwork, we're less likely to be seen. We don't have much time," Amy whispered.

They did not have to go far before they spied a utility door, and they slipped inside a maintenance room just in time, for the alarms had begun to wail.

"When you have poured the champagne, you may leave," Dr. Randall instructed his assistant. After he had watched her leave the office and close the door, he turned to the Patriarch. "Shall we meet with the Leader tonight, Your Eminence? Shall he reveal his plan to us? I am astounded that He condescends to come to us in the Patriarchal Center for Health Advancement."

"He is here already," said the Patriarch, although his mouth had not moved at all. His left eye glowed with a green light, and then his right eye. As smoke curled from his nostrils, the Doctor and the High Priest heard him say through closed lips, "He is with you always." The green mist continued to emanate from the

Patriarch, wafting in all directions, filling up the room from the floor to the ceiling, unnerving the priest and the doctor, for the vapor was so thick that it seemed they might suffocate in it. In the center of the miasma, a denser portion was separating itself, an emerald nebula in a sea of green gases. The nebula assumed a more definite shape, seemingly more concentrated, although not solid, in the style of a cyclone, which is and which is not a material mass. The three men prostrated their elegantly shrouded forms upon the floor—for they were in the presence of The Leader. They remained face-down, trembling as they heard the words of The Leader in their minds:

"Men of science, of government, and of faith, you are our creatures," they heard The Leader chortle. "Your sun is dying—this is the reason we have journeyed to this withering planet. Nocturnal creatures, moon-bred predators, fortified by the light of the glorious moon—we thrive in the night! We have come to this globe to cultivate a sustainable spring of human blood, for we live by imbibing the elixir of life! The time is short to discover the means—for the imminent demise of the sun shall bring about the extinction of your species. When the humans are extinct on earth, we shall hunt in other places."

"Hail, Blessed Diana, Huntress, Goddess of the Moon," chanted the High Priest.

"Priest—we are not your *gods*. We have naught to do with the moon or the sun. We are devourers of men. We are feasters in the charnel house. We are gourmands of misery. We want only your blood. You are simply our procurers. In the end, you will be our food and drink."

"Here, Jason, will this screwdriver help?"

He accepted the tool from Maggie:

"What else do you have in the knapsack?" was his grim attempt at levity. "There, it's getting loose. I've got it." He pulled the grate from the basement wall. "We can get into the exhaust system here. Let's go—quick!" Alice slid into the crawlspace, and then Maggie, and Jason closed the grate behind them after he was inside.

"I don't know what we'll do now that we're here, but let's get moving," he whispered. "Let's see what we can find out. Be careful, girls."

The trio crawled for at least thirty minutes, through pipes and tunnels.

Jason whispered, "Thank goodness the heat is not blasting—they must not be using this part of the building at present." When the pipes opened into a small, white-walled, windowless room, they carefully extricated themselves from their tight confinement and stretched their cramped limbs. Spying a discarded welder's torch in a corner of the room, Jason slipped it into his backpack, and then he heard faint sounds—they were coming from behind one of the walls. Hurriedly, he assisted Alice back into her hiding place. Maggie climbed in after her, motioning to Jason to follow. When he did not move, she looked at him questioningly.

Jason's attention was fixed on the opposite wall. Maggie had just about decided to give up on him and close the cover of the tunnel, when she heard Jason gasp.

"Joan!" he breathed, for he recognized the sound of her voice. As he watched, the metal plate on the wall began to wobble—and Joan emerged from the opening! Jason pulled his astonished wife to him. As Midge and Amy followed Joan out of the duct, Maggie and Alice came forth from the other wall—and the six refugees stared at each other in amazement.

They summarized their experiences with few words—they dared not linger to trade stories.

"First thing, I'll help all of you find a way out of this place," Jason told them. "And then I'm going to try to learn what they're up to." Joan looked distraught.

"Joan, I have to," he said, looking her in the eye. "I doubt that any of us will live much longer, but I want to fight the bastards. I just want to do what I can do. We don't really even know what we're up against."

"Jason, I'm not leaving you. I'll help you give them what-for —and then... And then, I'd rather die with you than without you. What's the point of a little more time—without you? Hiding from the moon, from the Patriarch, from other people... trying to stay alive another day? I want to help you."

"Jason," Alice said. "We're not letting you face them alone. Maggie and I are staying with you, too." Midge and Amy were not leaving him, either.

"What's out there, anymore? Alan is dead. It's always dark. It's always cold. And I'd have to hide alone somewhere," Midge said quietly. "There's nothing to go to."

Jason led the group through the labyrinth of ductwork. Holding their breaths whenever Jason paused, they crawled on their hands and knees, through a honeycomb of dark and cramped corridors hidden within the ceiling and walls. In the darkness, the company thought they could see Jason listening at a grate—and then, when a green light began to glow through the grille, they realized they were in the ceiling above an office. Jason doffed his backpack and withdrew the torch from it.

And then he abruptly kicked in the grate—and dropped through the ceiling into the green-fogged room. When he had gained his footing, he struck the Patriarch in the head with the torch—and then he turned on the flame, directing it at the three crow-like figures, who were shielding their heads with their arms!

"You bastards—you're not drinking my wife's blood! *You killed our child!*"

The mist was clearing, seeping out around the doors. Fire alarms were shrieking, like Banshees foretelling impending demise.

"No!" screamed Amy, as Joan jumped through the aperture

in the ceiling and fell to the floor below, beside her husband. The Patriarch was screeching insanely, his robes aflame, his head concaved and rhythmically spurting blood. The High Priest lay dead, a charcoal mess, his facial features melted into a sloppy gel by the flames of the torch. Doctor Randall was shrinking in a corner, holding his scorched arms before his face.

Joan picked up the lamp on the desk and began hammering him with it—and the Doctor latched onto her robe and pulled her to his side. He yelled to Jason, "Stop at once! I have your wife!"

Jason paused—he looked toward the corner, where the Doctor had hold of his wife.

"I have a syringe in my pocket. I will kill her if you don't let me out of here. Drop the torch."

Jason hesitated—and then he let go of the torch, and the flame went out. The door burst open—twenty armed men rushed into the room. The first to enter shot Jason between the eyes. Joan screamed—she struggled with the doctor to go to him.

"Stay, girl. I will kill you in a second."

She did not waver. She struggled to reach her husband.

"You monster—go ahead and kill me! There's nothing left to live for. My husband is dead! My baby is dead! The earth is dead! I'm not going to be your food. *Kill me!*"

She slid to the floor, as he withdrew his syringe from her side. In the crawlspace, the women could only gaze in horror.

Legends of Black Mountain

The Eyes Have It
Or, The Nurse of Black Mountain

From the doorway, the nurse screamed into the empty hall, "*Help!* Room 409. *Stat! Call 911!*"

She continued to scream for help as she ran to the bathroom. She turned on the water in the white ceramic sink, running it so it would become colder and pulled clean towels from the shelf. She soaked the towels in the cold water, pulled on a pair of gloves, and hurried back to the narrow, blood-soaked bed, in the center of which a middle-aged woman in a hospital gown drenched in her own gore was holding her eyeballs in her hands. The nurse softly pressed the wet towels to the woman's face. When the first persons entered the room, she sent one for ice and the other to call for an ambulance.

She heard an aide on the phone, "Yes, Shady Acres Nursing Home. Please hurry."

"The eyes are the windows of the soul," Kelly thought as she trudged through the blackened snow of the un-ploughed hospital parking lot. The phrase, which she had come across in a historical romance she had been reading the night before, was still reverberating in her mind. "*My* soul is covered in soot and snow, like the rest of Buffalo. Will spring ever come?"

"Did you hear Sharon got canned?" Angela asked her as she

approached the nurses' station, tracking black snow into the hospital. "501 complained about her."

"Yeah, and she was the only one working last night—everyone else called off, according to the staffing sheet," Kelly said, as she perused the grid on the clipboard. "I don't know how long I can put up with this. I've had enough!"

"They're all alike, you won't find a better job," Angela responded. "We're replaceable parts, you know. Blame us for everything, get a new part to replace an old, and you make the customer happy."

"I'm tired of snow. I'm tired of grimy Buffalo. I'm tired of this job," Kelly spat through gritted teeth. "Okay, give me report, Angela, so I can get started. I brought you a hazelnut coffee."

As the ruddy dawn struggled half-heartedly to penetrate the dour, lead-heavy sky, Kelly took a long last look at the black-grit-slush-covered two-lane boulevard which her apartment faced, and which was mottled, obscenely this morning, with the sopping, sickly-green papier mâché remains of the previous day's St. Patrick's Day parade. The air smelled of flat beer mixed with sleet. Kelly checked the hitch attaching her yellow Volkswagen Bug to the U-Haul and climbed into the cab, kicking the dirty slush from her boots before placing them on the clean floor mat. She was headed for the foothills of New Hampshire's Black Mountain, having accepted, through an agency, a private-duty position caring for a seventy-year-old widow living alone on a derelict farm twenty miles from the nearest one-horse hamlet on the eastern border of Vermont. Vermont was advertising for tourists to settle permanently in their state, their population being so low that they desperately needed workers; they were even offering incentives. To Kelly that sounded like Paradise.

As she drove through the ghoul-haunted Catskills, first east toward the sunrise, then north toward the top of the United States, she envisioned the thousands of pristine, industry-free acres of her new home. She shed herself of city, suburb, corporate health systems, litter, pollution, drug abuse, and the bane of her former life. She was going to Eden to begin anew. An old farmhouse, one patient, a lady on the wrong side of young, fir trees tall enough to blot the sun, unpolluted streams, wildlife, hard-working, independent Vermonters—Kelly had never felt so free, so fresh. As she approached the Massachusetts-Vermont border, she relished the loneliness, the height, depth, and breadth of the forest. The miles between the small towns along the road grew longer and longer, and, after only an hour in Vermont, just one out of three advertised a gas station or a restaurant at the exit. Kelly decided she had better fill up at every chance, not knowing when another opportunity would present itself. It was sunset when she arrived at Darkner Park and obtained from the caretaker the keys to her log cabin in the shadow of the distant and looming Black Mountain.

"Maybel Strachmire?"

A petite woman with a full head of shoulder-length grey hair that hung loose about her neck nodded. Keeping both hands firmly on the door, she held it open two inches and asked who wanted her.

"I'm Kelly Stuart, the Registered Nurse from Darkner Home Health. May I come in?"

"Come in, then. Kelly, you say?"

"Yes, Ma'am. Pleased to meet you. What a lovely home. May I put my bag down on the table? I'm afraid I must begin by asking a lot of nosey questions and filling in a number of forms for those pesky insurance companies."

"While you're going through your paperwork, Kelly, I'll get us some tea and cookies."

Maybel was a very independent old woman. She still did her own cooking and housework, but had a hard time keeping her heart medicine and cholesterol pills straight and on schedule. In bad weather, she was unable to get groceries. Kelly made all the necessary arrangements to help her with these issues, and she scheduled a return visit. Her heart singing with the contrast between her new life and her old, she walked to her car, congratulating herself on a wise career move.

Through twice-weekly visits in spring and summer, Kelly and Maybel became good friends, almost mother and daughter. Kelly would bring lunch and do regular check-ups on Maybel's blood pressure and her arthritis. Maybel's stories of mountain life half a century ago kept Kelly spellbound over chef salads and sandwiches with tea and Maybel's snickerdoodles. When summer turned to fall, Maybel's stories turned to mountain lore.

Kelly asked her about the mysterious stone circle at the southern border of New Hampshire, and Maybel knew all about it. It was supposed to have been erected before the arrival of the European colonists—even before the Indians ("Oh, I guess they're called Native Americans now, who can keep all these changing words straight?") settled the region.

"Who set up the stones?"

"Nobody knows," answered Maybel. "Some say the Vikings from Iceland. It's a mystery, is all I know."

"Did you ever see them?"

"Yes, my sweetheart and I—Zed, my late husband, that was —went a couple of times for a picnic on our way to vacation in Massachusetts."

"Was it spooky?"

"Well, kind of. You see, Kelly, we used to tell Halloween stories set in the stones around campfires."

It was thirty-five degrees and a roaring wind was blowing a stinging rain–snow mix of precipitation that *rat-a-tat-tatted* on the windows and whistled through the shingles, on the day Kelly was

71

dismayed to find Maybel struggling to breathe. Her friend had a high fever, and her chest was congested. Kelly gave Maybel some Tylenol and called an ambulance.

"Shady Acres? Hi, May I speak to Maybel Strachmire in 409? She's a good friend of mine. I used to be her home-health nurse—"

Kelly dropped the phone and stared at it, repeating "Oh my God, oh my God, oh my God—"

Kelly took a week's vacation, and she spent three days of it on the Maine coast. The eagles gliding over the harbor as she walked on the beach picking up shells made her think of Maybel, she couldn't think why, and that gave her comfort. What had made Maybel pluck her own eyes out? Had there been an undiagnosed brain tumor? A stroke? Insanity simmering below the surface? Poor Maybel. Kelly hoped that her friend was in a better place now, at least.

On her way back to Vermont, she detoured from the highway to visit the notorious stone circle secreted within the dense and eldritch forest of New Hampshire, of which so many weird stories were whispered around campfires. She paid her entrance fee and then hiked the woodland trails, enjoying the primeval forest for its own sake. Placards set up on posts along the way told of various conjectures purporting to explain the configuration of slabs and boulders on ledges and in clearings, or among the trees. Kelly wondered whether the stones were a naturally occurring formation, or if human hands had arranged them that way. Some of the signs described the astronomical orientation of the stones, which seemed to have been aligned with the solstices.

On Monday, she visited a new patient. Clara Clarke was only thirty-five, but she suffered from an especially insidious form of multiple sclerosis: she would be fine one day and totally helpless the next, without warning. Her husband had divorced her when she was diagnosed, and she was doing her best to live a worthwhile life, with the assistance of the home health agency, which would respond when she pushed the button she wore around her neck on a chain. Before she was struck, Clara had been the lead singer in an all-girl hard rock band on the verge of striking a record deal. Her mood varied between determination and bitterness, so Kelly never knew which side of her she would see on any given day. But her heart went out the young woman, who had been cheated by the roll of cosmic dice.

It was on a Friday morning when Kelly made her routine visit that Clara had failed to answer the door, either by opening it or by speaking through the intercom, which she did when she couldn't get to the door. Kelly called her name several times, with increasing urgency, but Clara did not answer. Finally, she drew her nail file from her purse and, sliding it between the screen door and the jamb, she lifted the latch and went inside. As she opened the door, Clara's grey cat raced out between her legs. Her heart beating a desperate measure, Clara went inside.

First, she threw up.

Then, she dialed 911.

"902 Hart Road, Putnam, Vermont. A thirty-five-year-old woman. She's—she's *dead!* She cut her eyes out! *She cut her eyes out!*

"I'll slow down. Hold on a minute," (sobbing).

"She's in her bed. She's got—she's got a knife—a knife—in each hand—and, and the knives—they're stuck in her eyes. Oh, god (retching)—I think she—she—chopped her eyes into mush . . .mush.

"There's blood—everywhere—

"Hurry!

"She's my patient—I'm her nurse—Kelly Stuart—from Dark-ner Home Care—Hurry, please!"

"I know you are in desperate need of help, and I'd like to help, but—I know I'll lose the $15,000 sign-on bonus if I leave before a year—I just can't..."

Despite her resolve to go back to Buffalo and to hire someone to sell her cabin for her in her absence, Kelly was talked into remaining in Vermont. After all, she must have exhausted her bad luck by now; and yet, she did not believe she would ever feel as comfortable and carefree as she had in March, when she ventured into her new life. She told the agency she wanted a month to recuperate before accepting a new assignment, and she spent August fixing up her cabin and her flower garden, bicycling, and taking long walks in the woods. She purchased a guide to indigenous flora and enjoyed trying to identify the plants she saw in the woods around her cabin. She signed up for an historical romance book club at the closest library, in Putnam County, just over the state line, where, perhaps, she could make a friend or two.

Elspeth Danforth could not walk. She had survived three heart attacks and a stroke and was pretty much stuck in her wheelchair or bed. Kelly arranged for frequent visits by nursing aides and visited herself three times a week, more often when needed. Elspeth had lived in the shadow of Black Mountain for ninety-two years, and she still had an active brain, sadly incarcerated in a useless body. Elspeth had never learned to read or write, but she retained facts like flypaper hangs onto flies.

"Poor Maybel. I used to watch her for her ma, when she went to work on the farms at harvest-time. She was a sweet little girl and grew up to be a smart lady. She opened a bakery on the highway, made good money selling to tourists who come for the fall colour or for skiing on Black Mountain in the winter. She expanded into souvenirs and made a good living for her family. Then she lost her husband and son to the Spanish Flu. But she stayed busy as ever.

"Did you know she came from Salem stock? She did genealogy, and we found out we were cousins, from way back when. In the sixteen hundreds, we both traced our roots to Ann Putnam. A stack of old family Bibles is the mother lode for genealogy.

"Come to think of it, Clara was our kin, too. It was nice when we found out we was related. Gave us a closeness we hadn't had before. Clara used to go to the library over the state line to research her family tree, that was before the M.S. got her. The Putnam tree is very big and spider-webery. I haven't thought about it in years. When you're an old invalid, you lose interest in some things.

"Ninety-two, yes, Ma'am! Hopin' to see a hunnerd, but maybe not, as the years don't get any kinder.

"Yes, I been to the stones. I went there the first time with a boy. He had such a sweet smile and a way of looking at a girl. After that, I learned not to trust 'em. Yes, he robbed me of my maidenhead—never could trust a man after that, not even my poor husband, 'though it weren't his fault. No, ma'am, it was too dark to see when it happened, but who else coulda done it?

"Maybel, too—her feller took what he wanted when they went to the stones. I guess it was a kind of lovers' lane, but it didn't feel like love after. I guess we were dumb kids. Live and learn. Yes, she said it was too dark to see what was happening or to try to get away—there was no moon that night because of heavy storm cloud cover.

"Oh, yes—Clara called the police, said she'd been raped there. Her fella had wandered off and left her to herself by a great stone laid on its side, and some strange man attacked her. She said it was pitch black by then and she couldn't give a description except that he had a lot of hair, and he was tall. She showed the police all the scratches on her. The police? Well, they said she musta enticed him somewhat, that some guys like it rough. Later, she married, and her no-good husband dumped her when she got sick.

"Aint' we the three! Never thought of it like that—Putnam descendants, and all three of us raped by the stones. Yes, Ma'am, we was all virgin-like when that happened. Girls got no sense sometimes when they like a guy. Live and learn."

Kelly stared at her hands in her lap. She was wringing them so hard that her nails were white. She looked Elspeth dead in the eye.

"You need to leave here. I was in Portland recently, on the Maine coast. I saw a real nice nursing home there when I was walking around town. It's near the water. I can get you moved there. You can't stay here! Three Ann Putnam descendants, three virgins raped at the stones, two dead—from gouging their own eyes out! *You must leave here at once.*"

Elspeth agreed, having nothing left to lose by leaving Vermont, and she moved to Eagle Shore Rest Home in Portland.

"I'll visit you on my next vacation," promised Kelly. "We'll have a nice lunch on the waterfront."

"Yes, that's right. I'm coming to see Elspeth on Wednesday, and I'd like to take her to lunch at the harbor, if that's all right. Exactly. I was her nurse in Vermont, and she's expecting my visit. I'll come to the reception desk at ten o'clock on Wednesday, then. Thank you so much. See you next week."

On Wednesday, Kelly arrived at the reception desk at nine forty-five, but there was no one there. She saw several people hurrying across the room, none of them paying her any heed. *There must be a code blue*, she thought, and waiting silently, trying to keep out of the way.

An ambulance pulling up to the glass doors confirmed her assumption, and she watched the EMTs as they hastily pulled the gurney from the back of the vehicle and raced inside and down the hall with it. Thirty minutes later, they rolled the sheet-covered gurney back through the glass door, lifted it back into the ambulance. A woman in a blue suit took her place behind the reception desk.

"May I help you?"

"Good morning. I'm Kelly Stuart. I've come to take Elspeth Danforth out to lunch. I believe they're expecting me."

"Ms... Stuart—please excuse me one moment."

A minute or two later, a man in a business suit came to the desk. "Kelly Stuart? Please come with me," he said, guiding her into his office.

"What's wrong? Has something happened to Elspeth?"

"I'm very sorry to have to tell you... I don't know quite how to put this, but... Mrs. Danforth has passed on."

"Was that her in the ambulance?"

"Yes."

"What happened?"

"She, um, well, since she had no kin, and since you're the only friend we know of, I'll tell you. She—she—she, um, pushed her eyeballs into her head with her fingers. We assume blood loss is the cause of death. But she has gone to the coroner. Did Mrs. Danforth have a history of psychological problems?"

He pulled up a chair and helped Kelly sink into it. She sat in silence for some moments, and then asked,

"Did anyone else come to see her? Did she say anything concerning?"

The answer to both questions was no, and the Administrator seemed dumbfounded, as well as sad.

Kelly managed to drive home.

For weeks, Kelly hounded the coroner, until she obtained the report. The elderly woman had been pregnant—with twins. One of the twins died in the act of devouring the other. Cause of death for mother and the twin who was still viable at the time of her death—blood loss. Only the tabloids would report this singular scoop, although it was public record.

After the moving van had gone, Kelly got into her car. The suitcases were already in the backseat. She stopped only to fill her tank at the first filling station off the freeway. As she pumped the gas, she could have sworn she heard the couple at the other pump saying, "The Mountain must have blood."

Black Mountain

*A*mbridge Carter started up the steep mountain, forging a path
through the old-growth trees and tangled brush. He had secreted his car
within a dense copse of trees, taking care to throw some fir-tree branches
on the hood and trunk, and then hiked away from the road—the only
road, as far as he was aware—up Black Mountain. As he dug the toe
of his boot into the soil and looked for branches to hold onto, he began
his ascent of the mist-shrouded mountain.

Carter had found his calling early in life, in the pages of the pulp
magazines he bought at the corner drugstore with his allowance, and
on weekends spent watching the science fiction and horror flicks at the
cinema or at the drive-in movie when the weather was nice. He wanted
to be one of those good guys—like Abraham Van Helsing—who root out
dark secrets and forbidden mysteries, and save the world. As an adult he
became an investigative reporter for the local newspaper, writing about
corruption in politics; later he wrote books on the Bermuda Triangle
and the Roswell incident. He wasn't sure what was going on with
this mountain, only that for years he'd been hearing about a string of
disappearances and hints of grisly details, never fully explained, never
corroborated. People sure did look over their shoulders when anyone
mentioned the mountain, though. Carter decided he would find out
what was behind all the innuendos and ambiguities. A fresh story
could be his big break, and so he had not told a soul where he was going.

There was a lodge at the top of the snow-capped mountain, an
expensive ski resort now, and the resort of bootlegging mobsters before the

Depression. Otherwise, there were only scattered houses, a few clustered in a couple of spots alongside the two-lane highway, close to the border that New Hampshire shared with Massachusetts, the rest isolated on farms or large wooded tracts. Service stations were fifty miles apart. He had passed one sign only, a battered plank swinging from chains and advertising a diner on a rutted dirt road that branched off from the highway. No wonder Black Mountain gave people the creeps: it was a solidly wooded mountain with one main road up and down it, a road that was walled in by trees on both sides that you couldn't see through or over, a road that wound so much that you couldn't see where you were going or where you had been.

Although still midday, it seemed the mountain forest was becoming darker. True, the sunlight had been barely able to penetrate the leafy canopy, even when he was driving up the winding road, and the mist, driveling rivulets down the curved glass, had made a veil of his windshield; yet it did seem that it was getting darker. Probably all in my head, Carter thought, Can't afford to get the jitters now. The vapor swirled around him.

He started to smell rot. He wished the light were better, but in the dim light the vegetation seemed green enough. Maybe the smell was because of the dampness caused by the fog. Good thing he'd started out in the wee hours of the morning, because it was only going to get darker from here on in. He continued to dig his feet and fingers into the mountainside. He clutched a stone to pull himself up on it, but it dislodged, nearly causing him to tumble down the incline. He righted himself and then looked at what he was holding in his hand—a bone—a human radius?

He eased himself into a groove, leaned back against a tree, and considered what he had found. When he got back to Boston he'd turn it over to the police, see what they thought. He doffed his backpack and bedroll, unzipped the backpack, and placed the grim relic among his foodstuffs and dry clothes. For another hour he climbed up Black Mountain. That was when he saw the opening of a cave. A good place for a rest, he thought, thinking he could record some observations in his notepad while he recuperated and imbibed an energy drink and a couple of granola bars. After he wrote about the mist, the darkness, the rotten smell, the arm-bone, and the isolation, he pushed his things behind a large rock and went further into the cave.

A bat, and then two more, flew swiftly past his head, causing him to duck. It was dark in the cave, and he had to use his mag light to look around. The usual stalactites and stalagmites, dripping walls—Whoa! the walls were carven with strange occult-looking symbols—and damp floors and—a shabby, brown leather briefcase! He vainly looked through his pockets for his cell phone to take pictures of the weird symbols. Damn! he must have left the phone in his car. Carter sat down and looked through the bag.

Files! Nine files labeled with people's names: "Kathryn Evans and Dr. David Campbell," "Evelyn," "Unidentified Hikers," "John and Amy," "Susan and Eben," "Alexandra," "Mr. and Mrs. Randolph and Anne Sanderson," "E. A. Darkner," "Joanna and Danielle," and a tenth file lacking a name.

Carter opened the first file, and as he read the narrative detailing the experiences of Kate Evans and Dr. Campbell on Black Mountain, his eyes grew wide and his flannel shirt wet with sweat.

The forecast was for snow, but as the winter had been, thus far, remarkably mild, Kate hoped that the meteorologist had been mistaken; and, while it was still possible to see without artificial light, and while the advent of darkness was, as yet, fifteen or twenty minutes in the offing, she ventured out to study the sky. Thick, rolling, old-mattress-stuffing, heavy, grey clouds, aligned themselves between the earth and the firmament. The cheerful, sunny, cold December day to which she had awakened—the winter solstice—was being routed by dark and portentous storm clouds that heralded the onslaught of a blizzard.

Kate called to her one-eyed grey tomcat, and he came bounding to her over the soggy ground. His furry feet were caked with wet mud layered over dried mud, and the tips of his straggly hair lightly were coated with the same: he had been exploring the sagging old chicken coops near the ramshackle farmhouse that was their new home. Kate chuckled whenever she thought, *I've just bought the farm.* No, for real: she had abandoned a cul-de-sac life for the remoteness of a derelict farm in New Hampshire, and a regular job for a go at being a full-time writer.

She experienced the world differently, she knew; she saw poetry in skies and enmity in weather. She would oft make pilgrimages between the covers of books—to cathedrals raised upon sweet phrases by the great architects of language. For her, words were exquisite jewels, wrought by master wordsmiths from the precious metals of the twenty-six letters of the alphabet. Kate, you see, dwelt in that mystical dimension inhabited by artists.

These poetic musings were halted by the wind, which was increasing in velocity. Scooping up Harry, Kate re-entered the house and braced herself for the onset of her first New England winter. She had laid in provisions for a couple of months—pens, paper, and books; she had secured the windows against drafts by tacking up plastic sheeting; and she had piled rugs against the doors. The stack of notebooks on her desk contained many detailed plans for conjuring her writer's retreat out of a farmhouse at the foot of a mountain—*a derelict farmhouse that had been abandoned forty years before*—when spring arrived. For the present, however, Kate was looking forward to the arrival of winter, to a period of isolation and repose, and to stoking her creative fires. She would reflect, consider, and conjecture, and put words on paper, perhaps to emerge in spring with a novel.

The nor'easter arrived at the farmhouse with howling gusts and thumped its shutters and fluttered its shingles and shivered its doors. Comfortable inside the old manse, Kate and Harry attended to the dramatic display. Kate was nestled in an overstuffed chintz chair, warm in her sky-blue Galway sweater and brown tweed trousers, her legs drawn up in the roomy seat; a glass of white wine was on the table, and a fire blazed in the hearth. She was attempting to read *Jane Eyre,* but Harry was competing with Charlotte Brontë for her attention, kneading her legs then burrowing in the space between Kate and the upholstery. And then his ears pricked, and his head turned toward the door at the same instant as Kate's.

Neither feline nor author could tell for certain whether there had been a knock at the door, what with the whistling wind and the banging of all the moveable pieces attached to the house; so the pair waited to hear if the sound would be repeated. A moment later they heard a rapping, quick and sharp, upon the door. Kate set her feet on the floor, and Harry jumped down and stood at attention.

Kate knew no one in her new neighborhood. The nearest town, Blight, was five miles away and was reached via the two-lane highway that snaked through the old-growth forest. The road was bounded on both sides by clear, sparkling, rapid streams drizzling down from the mountain. The further north one went in New Hampshire, the sparser the population, the fewer the towns, and the more isolated the homesteads. Although there were ski resorts higher up on the mountain, there were many acres which had never been cleared; within this wildwood, a thickly tangled mat of overhead branches impeded the pale moon's light, making the black of night opaque. Kate's closest neighbor on Black Mountain was a farm situated three miles in the opposite direction from the town, on the same dirt road that probably would not see a snow-plow until two days after the storm had ended. Except for the Realtor, and the contractors who had been updating the utilities and drawing up the blueprints, no visitor had been to Kate's home since she had moved in six weeks prior to the events of this night. Given these circumstances, a rap at the door in a snowstorm was an unsettling occurrence.

The side-blowing snow thwarted Kate's efforts to see outside through the plastic sheeting on the windows—and she found her-self wishing that the projected security system had already been installed. Finally she called, "Who is there?" Harry retreated under the end table, all the while maintaining his watch. No answer came to her inquiry, only the roaring of the wind. Kate placed her fingers gingerly upon the doorknob, her intent being to open the door just a little bit to peek out; but as she turned the knob, a violent gust pulled the door from her hands and slammed it against the wall. She moved to recover the doorknob and close the door—but the gale wind seized the opportunity to drive the blizzard inside.

Swirling flakes temporarily blinded her and coated the floor with snow, but Kate managed to secure the door and lock it. She saw that Harry had not moved a muscle, nor had he averted his fixed one-eyed gaze from the door. Her own dilated pupils darted wildly, searching for *something*. Crazily, the invading blizzard seemed a living—even malevolent—thing as it forced its way through the door. Kate experienced the urge to escape.

Quickly wresting control of herself from an encroaching, unnamable terror, Kate reproached herself for being a sorry New Englander, to be so easily spooked by a nor'easter. She deposited another log on the fire and poked around the coals, stoking the flames higher. She gave kitty treats to Harry and put the tea kettle on the stove, busying herself to exorcise her bad case of jitters; but only moments after she had located her place in her book Kate was surprised by a *new* pounding at her door.

"Hallo! Is anybody home?" followed the knocking. "I'm a lost traveler, and I'm in sore need of help. Please, answer—if you are there," continued the traveler as he recommenced his knocking.

Faced with a real person in real need of her help, Kate put aside her forebodings and opened the door to a portly individual of average height, whose other features were well hidden by a thick layer of white snow covering his person. She pushed her auburn hair from her blue eyes, where the wind had blown it, so that she could see the traveler she was letting into her home. Beckoning him into the house, she closed the door. The snow-covered traveler removed his fedora, which seemed more snow than hat; holding it in his hands, he spoke:

"Many thanks, gracious lady, for offering this weary traveler succor from the storm. My automobile is wedged in a snowdrift on the side of the highway, and I have trudged with heavy footsteps up the dark and lonesome road, till at last I saw your firelight in the window, which revived my flagging spirits. I shall never be able to repay your kindness." He took a breath. "I shall now introduce myself: I am David Arthur Campbell, and I became snowbound, snow-tossed, and lost at the foot of the mountain, up which I had intended to motor en route to a hostel curiously known as Top of the World, high up on the summit of the Black Mountain." And then he bowed.

"Certainly, you are welcome to come in from the blizzard. I am so very glad you found my house. Please, give me your coat and hat. Warm yourself by the fire. I am Kathryn Evans, and yon feline gentleman is Harry," Kate replied, smiling, as she helped the snow-covered stranger with his coat. When he heard his name, Harry's ears pricked, and with his one eye he scrutinized the traveler, now sitting in the lilac Bergère chair before the fire.

Kate brought from the sideboard a lacquered tray with a cut-glass decanter of sherry and two glasses, and she placed the wine on the yellow ottoman between them. The aspiring author seated herself across from the traveler and poured the sherry, telling him, "I have recently moved to the middle of nowhere so that I could concentrate on my writing with fewer distractions. What occasions your own journey through a treacherous nor'easter to the top of the dread Black Mountain, Mr. Campbell?"

Stretching his back, Harry meandered to the traveler, whose pants leg he began to sniff.

"Ms. Evans," Campbell replied, scratching Harry's ear by way of returning the feline's greeting, "it is *Professor* Campbell, but I answer to David, and I would like it if you would call me that. I am a professor of ancient occult religions; and I am here to join a group of respected scholars who have gathered from around the world to attend a conference on Lost and Forgotten Belief Systems. I am slated to lead a panel on Exorcism through the Ages, the day after tomorrow. I expect the road will have been cleared by morning, at which time I can have my vehicle pulled out of the snowbank and then resume the final leg of my journey—the ascent up the forbidding Black Mountain."

Intrigued, Kate leaned forward to begin plying the professor with questions—but then the lights flickered. "I hope we don't lose power tonight," she said. "In case of that eventuality, though, I have installed a generator in the shed behind the house, as well as a goodly stock of wine and viands to render being snowed in a tolerable predicament." Professor David laughed heartily and called her a spunky gal. He picked up his glass and tasted the wine appreciatively. For a few moments they sat together in silence, listening to the wind.

Kate confided that she was not always so spunky, having had quite a fright only moments before he arrived, when the snow had blown in so hard that she had been quite convinced that some *malevolence* had come in with it; but now she realized that the ferocity of the wind forcing the door from her hands had stimulated her imagination. "Maybe I should write a story about it," she said with a wry smile, "a *ghost story*."

The itinerant professor stopped grinning and, putting down his glass, asked Kate to explain in detail what she had experienced. She described for him the strange *rapping* at her door—"Oh, now I'm channeling Poe," she said, chortling at her own foolishness— and she told him of the violence with which the wind had forced its way into her home. As she refilled their glasses, Kate concluded her account with an admission that she had been merely suffering from a case of bad nerves in a blizzard.

"My dear," he leaned into her as he spoke, "you need not be so quick to discount your instincts, for you understand that there is as much truth in the immaterial as in the material. You would do well to give credence to the warnings of your psyche—several phenomena that you have enumerated cause me grave concern."

The professor was taking much too seriously the evil premonitions Kate had been trying to explain away with common sense, and she began to perceive the drawbacks of living in isolation. The authoress had been prepared for the challenge of rehabilitating a dilapidated farmhouse on a decrepit farm in an isolated rural area, but she was by no means ready to encounter the supernatural. Kate was about to insist that the professor admit he was making a jest at her expense, when the roar of an engine pulling up to the door and the sound of sturdy boots on the snow ended their conversation.

Kate opened the door to a man clad in a snowsuit and goggles, his purring snowmobile a few yards distant. He lifted his goggles to reveal his blue eyes and thick brown hair and said that his name was Paul and that he had been sent by the people at the lodge atop Black Mountain to seek a missing guest with whom they had lost contact in the storm, and whom they feared was lost in the snow. The scout was relieved to find the professor, and the professor was relieved to have been found. Kate was glad, of course, but her gladness was somewhat tempered by the effect of the events of that day and by their unfinished discussion.

"Dear Ms. Evans—"

"Kate," she said.

"Dear Kate, please accept my gratitude for your generosity to a stranger. I hope you will be my guest for dinner at the lodge, if the road is passable, tomorrow or the next day, so that we may resume our conversation. I reiterate that you *must* heed the warnings of your intuition. May I telephone you to inquire how you are faring?"

"I shall be delighted to accept your invitation, David, and I wish you luck with your presentation. It has been a pleasure meeting you, as well, Paul," she added, smiling at the snowmobile driver. She closed the door and heard them drive away as she returned to her place by the fire.

After a restless night's sleep, during which she had been awakened several times by odd noises and howling wind, Kate awoke to a cheerful morning sun pouring light into her bedroom. In the aftermath of the storm, the sun had reasserted itself in the light grey firmament, and its yellow beams were reflected brilliantly by the sparkling white snowdrifts; yet the air remained chill and below freezing, the wind continued to blow, and everything out of doors was buried beneath two feet of snow. The mundane sound of the snowplow, for the services of which she had prudently contracted, signaled a welcome resumption of normalcy. Kate let Harry out the door to take care of business, which he did lickety-split in the frigid snow, afterward quickly resuming his favorite place by the fire to give his attention to grooming his rough, grey coat. After she shoveled a path from the front door to the porch stoop, Kate prepared breakfast for herself and Harry. And then, placing her cup and saucer on the desk, she picked up her pen to ply her avowed trade of authorship.

As Kate labored happily at her novel, the glorious midwinter day passed much too quickly—and then darkness reclaimed the field. Making some quick notes of her ideas, Kate tidied up her desk and then snuggled in the chair near the hearth, as she had the evening before, intending to enjoy *Jane Eyre*. Instead of reading, though, she lapsed into a reverie, thinking on the weird events of the last twenty-four hours. Laying her book down, Kate rose and walked to a window; she pulled back the plastic to look at the weather outside.

A battalion of gloomy clouds had obliterated the moon and all the stars—and blackness only lay beyond the tiny zone illumined by the porch light. The universe seemed, in fact, to end at the edge of her porch—mere nothingness beyond. It seemed that to set foot off the porch planks might result in her leaving the world altogether.

From this primordial void came a soft sound, a rustling. Instinctively, Kate drew back from the window to avoid being seen. Realizing that she was shivering now—that the temperature was falling—she placed her hand on the radiator. It was producing warm air, and the fire continued to burn in the hearth; nevertheless, the air was so cold that she could see her breath. As the rustling grew louder, Kate returned her attention to the window.

Peering out into the inky blackness, she tried to determine the source of the rustling. The fluttering was becoming louder now—and yet even louder, coming closer and closer from the darkness, too. Kate placed her hands over her ears—feeling as if the noise would swallow her and the house as well. As the din became unbearable, her heart beat wildly. A dull *thump, thump, thump* on the roof—against the wall—and on the windows—sent her into a panic. The pounding of her heart and the percussion from without merged. Perspiration beaded on her forehead, dampened her armpits. The thumping came fast and hard—*thump, thump, thump, thump, thump*. Then it stopped.

Then there was no sound at all. No fluttering. No howling of the wind, no creaking of the house, no sound whatsoever except the thudding of her own heart. With her ear against the door, Kate listened, but she could hear nothing. She opened the door—and then she drew it wide. By porch light she could see piles of them—hundreds of crows. Black, feathery piles of crows. Dead crows. They were on the roof, and on the porch, and on the stoop. She would have to step on them to go outside.

In his suite at the Top of the World, Professor David Campbell was reviewing his notes for the presentation he would be giving the next day. A recognized expert in the field of occultism, the professor was a sought-after lecturer in university departments of comparative religion. As he buttoned up his charcoal vest and pulled on his grey tweed jacket, he anticipated lively debates about both ancient beliefs and the more recent proliferation of modern cult activity. He was thinking also of the delightful woman who had offered him shelter from the storm the previous night: in fact, he worried for her safety, given the macabre manifestations she had described. It was time for the welcoming banquet now, and David picked up his briefcase and headed toward the door. First, though, he thought he had better check on Kate. He put down the briefcase and picked up the phone to call her.

It took her a while to realize the phone was ringing. Somebody was trying, again and again, to reach her. Emerging from the haze that had once been her brain, Kate slammed the door shut and raced to pick up the French phone on the desk. With two shaking hands, she held the receiver to her ear and cried, "Hello! *Hello!*"

"Hello, Kate. I hope I am not disturbing you, calling so late." *It is the professor! David is on the phone!* Kate sank into a chair. David's voice on the other end of the telephone line was something akin to a life preserver tossed to a person drowning in a maelstrom and going under for the third and last time.

"Oh, Professor, oh, no, you're not disturbing me; in fact, I'm very relieved to hear your voice. I have had an awful scare—and you have called at just the right moment." She struggled to wrench the words from her constricted throat to her mouth.

"Are you all right?" David asked, his tone betraying worry. "Please—please, tell me what has frightened you so?"

Kate told David of the encasing, profound deep dark of the starless night—of the terrifying fluttering sounds—the ghastly mounds of dead birds—and the chill of the tomb inside the house: "Were it not for the horrible mounds of dead birds I would think I have gone insane and perhaps had imagined it all."

"Possession," was the professor's earnest response. "The house is possessed by an entity most foul. Leave at once. Hesitation could be deadly."

The telephone went dead, and Kate's frantic efforts failed to raise a dial tone. She let go of the receiver and it fell to the floor. Her chest rose and fell with short, quick, breaths—breaths that were evident in the frigid air. She felt the hair on her arms standing erect; she tried to figure out what to do. She pulled her coat, hat, and gloves from the closet, knocking several garments off their hangers in her haste, and then she placed Harry in his carrier and made for the door. Without bothering to lock it—not even hesitating to step over the piled-up bird carcasses—she hurried to the car, tossed the carrier into the back seat, and fitted the key in the ignition. But there was no sound, no rumble of an engine coming to life, no whine of an ignition trying to turn over, no dinging of warning lights. Just deadly silence.

The snow was falling again, gathering in intensity. The wind was raging; the car was rocked by the gusts. Kate had just decided to take Harry back into the house when he began to hiss and caterwaul, rolling and thumping around inside his carrier. Turning to look in the backseat, she watched as the carrier flipped over, saw Harry lying motionless within. She pushed open her door to get out of the car and check on her little pal—and a wind gust slammed the door into her body, knocking her to the ground. Face down in the snow, with her foot caught in the car door, the world dissolved.

They found her lying unconscious in the snow, her left foot caught in the car door, and Harry dazed and cowering in his carrier in the backseat. The professor had commandeered the Hummer and the driver, Paul, and they had left the lodge instantly when the phone had gone dead. The men lifted Kate up out of the snow and brought her inside by the fire. David pulled blankets from the bed, wrapped her up in them, and chaffed her hands and feet, while Paul rescued Harry. Paul prepared a warm bed of bath towels for the cat and laid him next to Kate. He then put a little sherry into a glass and poured some between Kate's lips, causing her to sputter to life again. "Oh, Paul," she cried, taking hold of both his hands, "where's Harry? Is he okay?" In answer, the mountain scout placed the swaddled cat in her arms.

"Oh, Harry, poor Harry, I love my sweet kitty, Harry," she

cooed as she softly kissed his battered body, her tears wetting his fur. Harry opened his eye and purred quietly, curled up into a ball in the towels in Kate's arms.

"Are you injured, Kate?" David asked as he gently pulled the blankets from her left foot. "Let me look at your foot." He lightly felt it, and Kate winced. "Can you move it?" he asked, and she did so, but it hurt dreadfully. Kate said that she thought it was not broken, but probably sprained. Paul went to the Hummer to retrieve an ace wrap from the first aid kit.

"That feels much better," she told the men after Paul had wrapped her ankle. "Let me have that glass of sherry now, if you please." After a long swallow Kate asked, "What should I do, David?"

"Come up to the lodge with us, Kate, recuperate, and then, in a day or two, you can decide what to do next, with a clearer head," answered David.

Kate gratefully accepted. Hobbling around, she gathered a change of clothes and necessaries, books and her writing, and supplies for Harry. Paul carried these out to his vehicle and alerted the lodge from the car phone, while David helped her walk to the door. She turned out the lights and locked the door, and then David helped her step over the mounds of dead black crows and assisted her into the car.

Paul expertly negotiated the steep trek up the icy mountain road and brought Kate and David safely to the summit, where a red-suited doorman with a handlebar moustache was awaiting them at the lodge entrance with a luggage cart and a wheelchair. Kate gave each of her rescuers an appreciative hug, and then the moustached doorman escorted her in the wheelchair, Harry on her lap, to the room that had been prepared for them. Philip, the concierge, explained to Kate that a desk clerk would come to her to complete the registration formalities, considering her situation, in the morning. He gave her a room service menu and said he had arranged for a doctor to visit her in the morning. Overwhelmed by the deference of the hotel staff, Kate expressed her appreciation.

"Nothing is too good, Ms. Evans, for a friend of Professor Campbell," replied Philip. "Please let me know what you require, and it will be our pleasure to accommodate your wishes."

Still rather dazed, Kate hung her clothes in the closet and unpacked Harry's things. After a steaming bath, she gave herself up to a numbing sleep among the crisp white linens and numerous pillows of the king-size bed. In the middle of the night, though, she wakened, sensing that someone else was in the room. She feigned continued sleep, endeavoring to stop her heart from galloping so loudly, afraid that whatever was lurking in the dark could hear it. Eventually she was able to persuade herself that no one else was there, and she rolled over and went back to sleep.

When morning came, Kate found the resilient Harry well on his way to recuperation. Kissing him goodbye and placing him in his carrier to keep him safe while the maid attended to the room, she ventured forth in search of breakfast. When she stepped out into the hall, she saw a raven-tressed maid hurrying away, and Kate wondered if the woman had been waiting at her door; and then, as she walked toward the elevators, she observed the same woman talking with another maid, further down the hall. The two maids turned from the utility cart they had been stocking and looked at Kate—at the same time—and then they turned away to resume their conversation. As the elevator doors closed, Kate noticed they were both looking at her again.

She limped to the registration desk and officially checked herself in to the Top of the World, and she asked the clerk to cancel the doctor, as her foot felt much better, and she was managing very well despite her injury. The marble and red velvet lobby was agleam with many brass accents; even the buttons on the bell-staff uniforms were made of brass. The sunlight spilling through the large glass entry doors caused a pair of massive crystal chandeliers to sparkle festively overhead. Kate felt detached from the terrors of the last two days on her farm—felt as if they belonged to someone else. Abashed that she had so overreacted to her first

New England blizzard—*the Nor'easter of 1999* she would term it henceforth—she felt humbled and determined to draw from this experience some measure of wisdom, along the lines of not overestimating herself in future. As she made her way to the restaurant, she became conscious of the other guests looking at her, and she wondered whether her limp was the reason that everyone seemed to be following her with their eyes.

Her self-consciousness increasing as she followed the breakfast room hostess to a vacant table, Kate tried to minimize her limp, for people ceased talking when she passed their tables, the chatter and clatter of the morning meal becoming a hush by the time she took her seat. After she had unfolded her napkin on her lap, Kate looked up. Not only was the room silent, but all eyes were upon her. Flustered, she turned her attention to the menu, and when the waitress came for her order, Kate asked her whether she knew why everyone was regarding her so intently? The waitress said she could only guess that Kate was the lone guest who was not registered for the conference: perhaps they were just curious about her reason for being there. As the waitress poured the coffee, Kate decided to accept this simple explanation, for she had already learned a painful lesson—in the form of a sprained ankle—of the consequences of letting her imagination run unchecked.

After enjoying a fresh croissant, tomato juice, and coffee, Kate signed the room check and took a newspaper to the grand lobby, where she intended to read for a while and perhaps spot David between conference sessions. She leaned back in an Italianate gilt and red velvet chair and caught a few words spoken by someone in a nearby cluster of people: "—from the farm."

She raised her eyes from the newsprint and turned them in their direction, but the people in that group were moving away. One or two of them turned back and glanced at her, as the group moved on.

Scanning the room, Kate caught a glimpse of a kiosk on which a conference schedule was posted, and she rose for a closer look. Among the many presentations and panels offered at the Conference on Lost and Forgotten Belief Systems were sessions on Biblical and pre-Biblical Possession and Exorcism, on Demonology and the Hierarchy of the Angels, as well as the Kabbalah. There were displays of fetishes, amulets, and various magical objects. One title drew her: *Black Mountain Magic.* It was scheduled to begin at ten o'clock, and it was now nine forty-five. Kate decided to see whether she could obtain admission. When she arrived at the room designated for the presentation, there was no gatekeeper, that is, no one checking registration. The room was full of people reading their programs or talking to their neighbors. Not seeing any one in charge to ask for permission to sit in, Kate took an empty seat in the back of the room.

The lights were dimmed, except at the podium in the front of the room, where a tall woman in a slim black pantsuit, her blonde hair pulled elegantly on top of her head, was arranging a sheaf of papers and saying words of welcome to the audience. Her steely black eyes surveyed the room and contrasted with the matte blood-red color on her lips as she spoke:

"I bid you welcome, colleagues," she began. "We have convened from the four corners of the earth, and from everywhere between, to pool our knowledge, to increase our power. This conference has been marked by outstanding academic contributions. Through these studies we learn to harness our gifts and hasten the time of Reckoning. To this end we have convened at dreaded Black Mountain, the dwelling of the Dark Unseen.

"We are all familiar with the sacred history of the mountain, and its thirst for blood sacrifice. Note the aerial view on the projection screen, the dark, jagged edges, the razor-like crags, the mountain's awful majesty. Note the altar at the mountain base, a wide and level field where blood-drenched crops are raised. Recall the story of the two English scouts who were mapping territory during the French and Indian War. The English governor was offering rewards for Indian scalps. In a raid upon a sleeping Indian camp, a maiden was stolen from her family and brought to this altar. They say her screams can be heard to this day when the wind is still. One scout held the girl while the other removed her scalp with a hunting knife, and then they continued to flay the flesh from her bones. Intoxicated by their gruesome activity, they painted their bodies with her blood, smearing themselves in imitation of Indian war paint. The maiden's mutilated body was tossed into the well, and the water at the altar still retains a reddish cast."

After the applause died down, the woman continued.

"Another well-known event took place during the American Civil War. Descendants of Salem Burning Times refugees had made their home at the altar at the foot of Black Mountain, where they survived by marketing their notoriety: they worked as mediums and astrologers. Strange fires could be seen during black nights, especially at the solstices. Local mountain dwellers came to them for potions to cure disease and find love, which they purchased from the pox-marked descendants of the Putnam family, until one day when they were all found dead: Putnam abdomens had been torn open, and Putnam viscera had been pulled out, spread all over the ground, and covered with maggots and a viscous black substance. The land was afterward abandoned for a generation: the mountain had been fed."

The audience eagerly awaited her next words. She moved to the front of the podium.

"Distinguished guests, hearken. I shall tell you a beloved tale, a tale of a more recent time, of our era and our own remembrance:

"You will recall how the John Deere monster, reptilian green and bloodthirsty as a Brothers Grimm dragon covered with scales glistening in the noonday sun, with glowering headlight eyes, with fiercely grimacing grill, rolled on its thickly treaded tires. It crushed the plants. It imprinted its deep tracks in the soil. It rolled past the man inspecting the hay that was ready for reaping, and the man looked up into the cab to see who was driving, and he saw that it was empty. The man ran after the tractor and tried to jump on board, tried to reach the controls. He held tightly onto the unfeeling, cruel metal, but he could not sustain a foothold, and he fell into the machine-made rut in the soil. He jumped to his feet and took off after the metallic beast again.

"Farmer John Sterling had been calculating the profits from this year's harvest when his pleasant ruminations were interrupted by the approach of the runaway tractor: it was the harvest of 1959, when the farm would finally turn a profit. Now, however, he forgot all about harvests and money as he ran, panting, over the uneven ground, to catch the runaway combine. Past the tractor—and in its path—was the farmer's four-year-old daughter, Amy, who was waving her arms at him, her blonde pigtails flopping, what with her jumping up and down, and she was calling, *Hi, Daddy!*"

The woman paused, smiling, as the audience tittered.

"*Run!* he yelled, as he jumped onto the combine again. *Get out of the way!*"

The audience cheered.

"As if he had been riding an unbroken bronco, instead of a mechanical combine, the farmer was thrown to the ground. He heard Amy's screams before he saw the blood. It was positively raining blood. John screamed, *No!* and other horrible things for which there are no words in the vocabulary of any human language, and he fell to the ground. Sobbing over the strips of jagged flesh and pool of thick, warm blood, and scraps of clothes and shoes, which were what remained of Amy; sobbing so intently that his body wracked with pain, he did not notice the combine until it rolled right up to him, just before it ground him into fertilizer for his crop."

There were calls of, "Hear! Hear!"

"After the funeral, Sterling's widow defaulted on the mortgage and moved to another state to be with her relations. The farm sat vacant and decaying. At first, curiosity seekers came around for a peek, but other people stayed away from it: it gave off a funny feeling. Even birds and rodents tended to circle around it rather than pass through. Only the spiders seemed to feel at home, industriously spinning their webs in all the corners. The dust grew thick on every surface, and the farm just mouldered and withered. In time it was forgotten, except as the stuff of local legend, the kind of house people told one another to stay away from."

The audience gave a standing ovation. The speaker patiently awaited the end of their applause, and then said, "I am gratified that you have enjoyed the story. I have one more point to make. The next slide is an aerial view of the altar today. The land is still laid out as a farm: note the Pentacle formed by the arrangement of house, barn, outhouses, and driveways. It is to this altar that we have come to offer the next blood sacrifice. The way has already been prepared. Winged black birds of hell, the crows that are the royal messengers, have come before the King of Darkness to announce his approach."

The slide was a picture of the mounds of dead birds on Kate's farm.

Autopilot mechanisms hardwired into Kate by evolution pumped adrenalin through her body. As the audience stood to salute the speaker, she rose from her seat, backed unobtrusively toward the rear of the room, and quietly slipped out the door. She threaded the halls of the conference wing of the lodge toward the guest rooms, endeavoring to appear calm and praying that she would not run into too many people. But even though there were very few people scattered about the halls and public areas, Kate spied the same brunette maid who had been at her door when she left her room earlier that morning. The maid was taking linens from the utility cart in the hall into a guest room, and Kate hoped she hadn't been noticed by her. At last reaching her room, she entered and locked the door, then sank onto the foot of the bed.

She knew she had to decide quickly on a course of action. She had to get away—but her car was still on her farm at the bottom of the mountain. A taxi seemed the most obvious recourse, and so Kate gathered minimal essentials in a roomy quilted tote bag and added a couple of towels from the bathroom. The last thing she put into the bag was Harry. She thought it would be better if it was not obvious that she was not planning to return, and therefore left the remainder of her belongings behind, with Harry's carrier. Kate put on her coat and boots and walked to the lobby, grateful that recent experiences had left Harry subdued, so that he would not attract attention as she carried him in the bag slung over her shoulder.

As she approached the main entrance to find a cab, Kate observed a snowmobile parked in front of the glass doors. Glancing toward the bellhop stand, she saw a key ring on the marble counter: snatching the keys, she hurried out the door, sat on the snowmobile, and tried the ignition. *It started.* She put her bag, with its precious cargo, into the storage compartment and took off.

It was a very jumpy ride, Kate never having driven a snowmobile before, but she seemed to be figuring out the machine well enough. She didn't know where she was going, only that she had to get off the mountain before it was too late. She drove as fast as she dared on the icy downward path—*five minutes, six minutes*—and began to feel that safety was within reach. Desperation was beginning to yield to hope. She had only to make it to a house, or a business, somewhere where there were people, off the mountain. As she rounded a curve, she saw the flashing lights of a roadblock. She applied the brakes and tried to steer away from the orange barrels, but the snowmobile slid sideways and plowed into the snow-filled ditch, coming to rest at an angle.

Kate was not hurt. She got off the snowmobile and checked on Harry. He was shivering in the storage compartment, but he did not appear to be injured either. Kate tried to move the snowmobile, but she couldn't budge it. She slung her bag over her shoulder and started walking downhill. She had only gone about thirty or forty feet when a police cruiser pulled up next to her, its lights flashing.

"Heavens to Betsy, Ma'am," the officer said as he stepped out of the car, "what are you doing walking down the mountain road in this weather?"

"I was headed back home, Officer," she replied. "I live at the bottom of the mountain. My snowmobile slid off the road a little way back."

"Well, Ma'am, this is pretty rough weather for outdoor sports, and it's a tricky road. You're lucky you didn't roll down the mountain." He opened the door of the backseat and said, "Please, Ma'am, get inside with me, and I'll see you get the rest of the way home safely. The road and all the trails out of here are closed now. We've had an avalanche. You'll probably get a kick out of this: folks who grew up hereabouts will be saying the mountain gods are angry," and he guffawed, "but you not being a local, you probably would think such talk stuff and nonsense."

"Officer, thank you very much," Kate answered, "but, honestly, I'm not that far from home, and I can make it on foot."

"No dice, Ma'am. I'd have to answer for it if anything happened to you. For your safety I'm going to have to insist on conveying you home in my cruiser, safe and in one piece."

"Well, I don't mean to seem ungrateful. I just didn't want to impose."

"No imposition at all, Ma'am. Officer Johnston at your service. Glad to help a fair maid in distress."

He helped Kate into the backseat, closing the door behind her. He turned the car back onto the road, radioed the police station, and asked Kate for her address. "The old Sterling place, you say," he responded. "You probably got quite a deal on that farm. It's been abandoned since before I was born. You gonna be a farmer, Ma'am?"

"No, sir. I'm a writer and moved up here for the peace and quiet, and the beautiful country."

"Well, Ma'am, you certainly chose well for beautiful country. Here you are, Ma'am, safe and sound as I promised. Let me see you to the door and make sure you're safely locked inside your house. It is wild weather, this is."

He helped her out of the cruiser. Kate held tightly onto her bag and got out, heading toward the front porch. As she and Officer

Johnston reached the door, the Hummer from the lodge pulled up behind the cruiser.

Paul and David emerged from the Hummer and joined Kate and the officer on the porch. "Kate," said David, "I couldn't find you and wanted to make sure you were all right. I was concerned that something had happened."

"I'm sorry I didn't say goodbye, David. I hadn't seen you around the lodge to tell you I'd decided to come home. I planned to call you later to thank you for all you've done for me," and she reached out to shake his hand, "And you, too, Paul," as she shook his hand, too. "Thanks to you, as well, Officer Johnston. Now I'll be going inside to warm up a little. Please, let's keep in touch," and Kate turned to go into the house.

David said good-night and turned to go, but Paul stepped forward to open the door for Kate and said, "I insist on making a good fire for you before we leave. Professor Campbell, why don't you help Ms. Evans put on a pot of coffee and thaw her out while I get the fire going for her?" David hesitated, and then passed through the door, which Paul was still holding open. Paul picked up an armful of logs from the porch and brought them into the house.

Inside the house, Kate released Harry from the bag, whereupon he immediately darted under the bed. Curled up into a ball, he squeezed tightly against the wall and fixed his one-eyed gaze on the bedroom door. The roaring fire burned down and the pot of coffee was drunk, during which interval Paul had maintained a steady stream of conversation, commenting on the weather and the bustle at the lodge with the conference, and asking Kate about her plans for the farm and the book she was writing. David, however, was curiously quiet, seemingly preoccupied, and not really following the conversation. Kate stood up and told her visitors that she was tired and needed to lie down for a while. She was saying that she did not wish to appear rude or unappreciative—when a muffled buzz or humming noise drew her attention. Kate turned around and cocked her head, attempting to locate the source of the sound.

Paul observed Kate's expression and said to her, "You hear that, too, don't you? Is your generator running? Perhaps your furnace is acting up?"

"The furnace was just maintained when I moved in, not quite two months ago, and the generator should not be running right now. Yes, I heard the noise, and I too, was just wondering what it is."

"I think it's coming from that direction," said Paul, and he pointed to the door at the back of the house. "I'll go outside and look around a bit. Check it out." He put on his coat and went out the door.

David quickly crossed the room to Kate's side. He said, "I have to tell you something. Get your coat. Quickly. We must get out of here. Now." Following her instincts, she picked up her coat from the back of a chair and put it on. David took her hand and was pulling her toward the front door when Paul came in through the back door.

"Where are you going? I think I found out where the noise is coming from. It seems there is a root cellar at the back of the house, and it sounds like there is something making some weird sounds down there. David, come check it out with me. Ms. Evans, you'd better come, too, and bring your keys, in case the door is locked, or something. Bring flashlights, too."

"I do not think it is such a good idea to go into a dark root cellar right now," protested David. "Ms. Evans is only just recovering from a sprained ankle, and who knows what is down there, in the dark. Why don't we just allow Ms. Evans to go to sleep and check on her in the morning? She's really exhausted right now and does not seem up to any more adventures today."

"You are quite right, David," Kate said. "I think the investigation had better be postponed until tomorrow. I am worn out. You guys have been absolutely wonderful to worry about me so much, but now I'd really like to hit the hay."

Paul answered, "Ms. Evans, I can't in good conscience leave you here alone with that unexplained humming. I must at least take

Professor Campbell with me, to check it out, and make sure nothing's going to explode or catch on fire or anything after I've gone. Come on, Professor, let's go to the cellar." Paul gripped David's elbow and steered him out the door. "We'll be back as soon as we've made sure it's safe, Ms. Evans. Just hold tight." And Paul, his hand on David's arm, walked out the back door with David, and shut the door behind them.

Kate seized her keys and fled out the front door, leaping over the dead crows, and with a shaking hand she inserted the key into the car door.

"Hey, Ms. Evans," she heard, and she turned to see Paul standing behind her. "Are you going somewhere?"

"No, Paul, I just needed to get something from the car. I'm too tired to go anywhere tonight," Kate said, trying to breathe normally with her heart beating like a sledgehammer on her ribs.

"Ms. Evans, David sent me to tell you to come down and see what we found. Here, let me take your arm, so you don't trip over this pile of dead crows. Weird, isn't it, all these birds dying around your house?" and Paul walked her back to the front porch.

He guided her into the house and, once inside, toward the back door. Kate tried to pull away, but Paul tightened his grip. "It won't take long," he said, "and then you will get your good night's sleep." By this time Paul was pulling Kate out the back door as she was trying desperately to keep from going through it. At the door they were joined by Officer Johnston.

"Hello, Ma'am," he said. "Nice to see you again."

"Johnston, hold onto the lady's other arm. She sprained her ankle, and she's a little unsteady. I was just helping her out the door. There's some noise in the root cellar, and we're on our way to check it out."

Officer Johnston held tightly onto one arm and Paul the other, and Kate was walked to the root cellar door and down the steps.

"It's us, Philip," Paul said, and the concierge from the mountaintop lodge opened the cellar door from the inside. Instead of a red uniform, though, he was wearing a black cowl and long black robe.

Paul pushed Kate inside. Philip followed and pulled the door shut behind him. Johnston stationed himself outside the root cellar door. Kate's knees gave out, and she sank to the ground, but Paul and Philip jerked her back up on her feet. Kate screamed—the cellar was lit by candles, dozens and dozens of them, red candles dripping hot red wax down black iron sconces and candlesticks! When Kate's eyes had adjusted to the candlelight, she was able to make out the black cowled figures standing around the perimeter of the cellar. In the middle of the room there was a white circle on the dirt floor, a five-pointed star in its center. The dark figures resumed their interrupted chanting: "She must have blood. The mountain must be fed. Blood unto blood. The mountain will have blood." The two men held Kate up on her feet.

The circle of black-cowled figures parted, revealing the woman who had given the presentation on Black Mountain Magic at the Top of the World that morning. She stood with head bent and arms folded in front of her. Raising her head, she ceremoniously spread her arms wide. Feathered black wings had grown in place of her arms, and her hands had become talons. Her red lips parted, and she laughed, a deep, sinister laugh. It was a deadly laugh—mirth laced with terror and pain. Despite the stillness of the cold air, the feathers on her wings fluttered. At her feet lay David, his face covered in blood. Two great black birds were plucking the eyes out of his head. Kate could not tell if he were alive or dead.

Two women came forth from the group, and the men handed Kate over to them. Each of the women took Kate by the hand. The blonde bird-woman stepped forward slowly into the white circle, and the two women led the terrified Kate toward her. The people around the circle continued to chant, "Blood. Have blood. She must have blood," and the bird-woman ran her tongue over her red lips. Philip approached the bird-woman, holding before him a crimson velvet cushion, on which lay a silver ritual knife, with a handle of black ebony fashioned into curving twigs, and a blade very sharp and glinting in the candlelight.

The golden-haired bird-woman spoke: "The Mountain will have blood." Motioning her wing toward David, she continued, "The Mountain lays low the enemy, David Campbell. The Mountain will have blood. The crows that are the royal messengers pluck out your eyes, and your blood fertilizes the altar. The day of reckoning draws nigh."

She turned to Kate: "Today, the unholy solstice, your hot blood shall fertilize the altar. Steam shall rise when warm blood drenches frosted earth."

Philip raised the crimson cushion. The bird-woman stepped toward him, reaching for the knife. Kate stared in terror, her hands held fast by the two black-garbed women. The robed figures continued chanting their mantra, the tempo of the chant increasing. Trembling, Kate awaited the gruesome death which was imminent.

"Aaggh!" came from behind her. The bird-woman and everyone else turned their heads. Harry was clinging to Paul's face with all the claws of his four cat feet. Paul tried to pull Harry off, but Harry dug all twenty claws in as deep as they would go and ripped chunks of Paul's face off with his teeth. Another robed figure came forward, pulled Harry off Paul's now-pulpy visage, and threw him across the room. In the commotion Kate pulled her hands free and seized the knife from the cushion that Philip still held before her. With a forward lunge of her whole body she plunged the blade into the bird-woman's chest.

The cellar filled with hot, black smoke, and then flames burst from all sides. Robed figures poured forth from the door. One cowled person picked up Harry and pushed Kate out the door into the snow. Another was dragging David out of the cellar by his arms, just as the ceiling caved in. The two robed rescuers pushed their hoods back and dropped to their knees, coughing, trying to fill their smoke-filled lungs with air—and Kate recognized the two maids whom she had seen at the lodge, in the hallway by her room. She ran to David—he was still alive, but his swollen face was bruised and bloody. She put handfuls of snow on his face and dressed his eyes with fabric ripped from her blouse. She went to find Harry, who was lying still and limp in the snow, his breathing labored. Kate lovingly took off her coat and gently covered him in it. Harry opened his eye halfway and purred weakly, and then closed his eye again, and drew his last breath.

As the fire engines arrived, Kate knelt in the snow by her beloved Harry, weeping in the agony of her grief, the sorrow for which there is no balm. Pounding her fists in the snow, she *wailed*. Her best friend was *gone*—he had given his life to save her. The house burned to the ground, but Kate did not know it, for she was immersed in her sorrow.

In the autumn Kate sat in the solarium of the rehabilitation hospital in Portland, Maine, rocking in a white wicker chair before a large picture window that overlooked the shimmering blue water in the harbor. She held David's hand in both her own. Her eyes became misty, and a tear slid down her cheek.

"It's very good news that you will be going home soon," said Kate. "I'm so glad your vision has improved sufficiently so that you can read and write, even if you have to wear a soda-bottle monocle, David. Actually, it makes you look even more distinguished. Not to mention the intriguing eye patch, which lends an air of mystery."

"Well, I have no left eye at all, Kate, just a socket. I must be grateful that an eye patch is considered an handsome accessory. And I am very pleased to have enough vision left to read. I shall be going home with my new friend, Cerberus, my seeing-eye dog. We are already great friends. I am profoundly happy that you have been left unscathed—physically, I mean."

"Yes, David, physically I am unscathed, and that is thanks to you and Harry. I miss him terribly. I would have died a horrific death had not you and the other special agents risked your lives to expose the cult. I owe you my life."

"I had no idea of the unholy ground I would be treading when I accepted a fact-gathering assignment for a government agency that is investigating cultism. I am, after all, a student of obscure ancient religions, not a detective. It was at the conference at the Top of the World that I first learned their plans—as well as the fact that Elizabeth Darkner, the owner of the lodge, was the high priestess of the cult of the Dark Unseen. Unfortunately, they found *me* out as well. I would not have brought you there had I known of the danger. I found out, too late, that I had entered a trap. Your blood and mine would be fertilizing the altar right now if special agents Victoria and Carolyn—who, I must admit, did a splendid job posing undercover as chambermaids—had not come up with the ingenious plan to save us by burning the house down right around us. It was an effective diversion, to say the least."

"Is it all over now, David? Really over?" asked Kate, squeezing his hand.

"Unfortunately, there is much more to it than that, Kate," he replied. "Although some members of the cult died in the fire and others have been arrested, the body of the bird-woman has never been recovered. The dread Black Mountain demands blood sacrifice to fertilize the altar. It is true the mountain has been fed, for now, with the blood of its own priesthood. But in time the Dark Unseen will hunger again. The mountain must have blood."

"How are you today, Professor?" asked the nurse who had just entered the sunroom. "You'll be leaving us soon, I hear."

"Kate, allow me to introduce my nurse, Julia. Hello, Julia, this is my friend Kate."

"How do you do?" Kate answered, looking up at the nurse's name badge. "Portland is an enchanting town. Did you grow up here? Is your family from Maine?"

"Yes, I grew up in Portland. My mother's family is from this area, but my father's side live in New Hampshire. As a matter of fact," she added, "my father's cousin owns a ski lodge in the mountains up there. Take care, Professor. We'll be sending our home health services to see you when you have returned home to New York."

As soon as Julia had left the room, Kate stood up and wrung her hands. She turned to David. "David, I know you have limited vision. Have you ever seen your nurse's name badge? It reads: Julia Darkner, R.N."

"When I get back to Boston I'm gonna have to look these two up!" he breathed out loud to himself. "What a find! A modern-day cult that kills people and sacrifices them to the mountain! I'll break the story all over the world."

Carter stood up from the cold, wet stone, stretched his legs, and walked to the wall. Shining the beam of his mag lite on it, he studied the dripping carvings, or graffiti, or whatever it was. He started writing in his notebook: birds, wings spread, pentagrams, skulls, and triangular mountain peaks. The euphoria of discovery began to subside as it dawned on him that he might be in danger if he were to be discovered here by the cultists. Secreting the empty briefcase in a lightless recess of the cavern, he hurried with the files back to the entrance. He placed the files in his knapsack, pulling out the dry socks and underwear to make room for them; those he stuffed in his coat pockets. Then he replaced the knapsack and bedroll on his back and resumed his climb.

He climbed for an hour, seeing nothing as interesting as the cave, but he could no longer resist reading the second file.

Evelyn of the Wood

Evelyn was driving home from her midnight shift as the front desk manager at the Top of the World, a boutique hotel perched precariously upon the side of Black Mountain, in the northernmost regions of New Hampshire, almost to Quebec. The rocky, wind-swept mountain draws visitors who enjoy the feeling of solitude in nature. The setting always made Evelyn think of Birnam Wood, which, in *Macbeth,* comes to Dunsinane: the wood seemed alive to her.

The forests of New Hampshire have never ceded ownership of the land, where human endeavor always seems to be a species of trespassing. The woods hem the roads that transverse the sparsely populated state and limit the views on either left or right to the prospect of trees, streams, and the pavement of the road; the narrow lanes wind snake-like through mountainous terrain, so a motorist can see neither beyond nor behind the next curve. The woods speak to those who will listen, in the rustling of leaves and the creaking of branches, as the wind strums the trees like lyres. Birds and small mammals, and smaller reptiles, flap and slither among the foliage.

Clearings this far north are few and far between. Occasional farms, general stores, and combination service stations/restaurants appear as small cankers upon the sentient landscape. These tend to smallness, as if ashamed of their interloper status, and as if they are begging one's pardon for being.

Black Mountain possessed the power to lull Evelyn effortlessly away from her thoughts of reservations and vacancies, room service, and plumbing considerations. The cares of her day would dissolve when she returned to her home concealed among the loving limbs of the trees. She could no longer remember the day, so long past, when she had sworn off human affection, having received the last hurt she could endure, from unfeeling parents and callous lovers. She had looked to the trees for solace, and they beckoned her into the wood. Beneath their boughs she licked her wounds and withdrew into herself until she emerged a new Evelyn, born of the dark forest.

Her meager savings she had spent on a narrow strip of land, upon which she had built a three-room cottage. She hung lace curtains in the small windows and prepared simple fare in the little kitchen. She gathered herbs from the abundance of her forest and vegetables from a small garden behind the house. To earn the money required for her humble existence, she worked the grave-yard shift at the Top of the World, a private resort that, rather than trespassing, seemed to have sprouted organically from Black Mountain. The mountain loved the lodge, and for that Evelyn honored it, too. She went to work at the hotel as a vestal virgin would have guarded the sacred fire of the Eternal City.

As her car approached the hidden dirt lane that linked her diminutive asylum to the road, she raised her eyes to the rearview mirror and put on her turn signal. Not often, but every now and then, there would be a driver with whom she was sharing the road when she descended the mountain after work. As she depressed the brake pedal, Evelyn twisted her neck to look in back: although, *now,* she could not see anything behind her, not even a headlight in the unlit road. She was certain she *had* seen movement in the mirror, a blur, a *face.*

She was relieved when she reached her cottage, her momentary fright receding amidst the trees. The first thing she did, once she was inside, was draw water for a bath in her clawfoot tub. As the bathtub was filling, steaming the mirror, she reverently removed the red jacket and skirt and the white blouse of her uniform, which ensemble, for Evelyn, served as sacramental vestments in the solemn performance of her obligations to the mountaintop lodge. She lowered herself into the hot water and soaked until her skin was pink with heat. Ready for bed, she pulled out the rubber stopper and got out of the tub. She crossed the small space to the tiny washbasin and began to comb her hair before the mirror—and then she whirled around to look behind. There was nothing there, save the antique bathtub and the dampened towel draped over its side. Turning back to face the mirror, she glimpsed a fluttering, which was slipping behind the mirror's beveled edge, and the shadow of a mouth.

Evelyn dreamed all night of mirrors. She kept looking in mirrors in gold rococo frames, magnifying makeup mirrors, and oval mirrors framed in mahogany, but, instead of her reflection, she would see trees. When she woke, she was glad that she did not have to work that day at the lodge, but could remain within her sylvan bower.

She broke her fast with bread and coffee and then walked among the elms and firs. She ran her hands along the trunk of one elderly tree, a great stout fellow of many rings, as tall as a skyscraper. She shivered as she felt the roughness of the slices of bark against the softness of her palms, and she counted all the shades of black and grey and brown in a little section of bark. She caressed the moist, many-veined green leaves, passed them over her cheek, and inhaled their perfume. She embraced a sapling, encouraging it to grow as tall as its parent.

By her hunger only Evelyn knew that the sun was high in the sky, for the wood permitted few rays of the golden orb to enter it, and she returned to the cottage for a luncheon of fresh tomato sandwiches on home-baked bread. She carried these outside, to dine beneath the leafy ceiling of her cloistered banqueting hall. She carried a volume of Thoreau, too, and she sat down upon a mossy log to read the verses of the kindred spirit, with whom she shared a wonder of the wood.

When she had sat long enough, she walked among the inter-laced trees, stepping with caution over the prickly bushes and far-reaching roots and climbing over fallen branches and great elms. The trunks of some very venerable trees, which had in death fallen to their sides, were too massive for her to clamber over, and their felled treetops were such multitudes of tangled branches that she could not pass through them; when she came to one of these great corpses, she had to walk the length of the form and around one of its ends.

The filtered light growing dim and the air becoming cool, Evelyn turned her steps toward the path of her cottage, knowing that she must be back before sunset, lest she be lost in the dark overnight. On her way home, she came to a pond that she had not seen before. Its stagnant water seemed aflame with the ruddiness of the setting sun, which had seized its opportunity to enter there—a breach in the fortification of limbs above. Knowing that there were nearly two hours of daylight remaining, Evelyn sat down at the water's edge to read her book by the red glow—and then a rippling in the water stole her attention from Thoreau. She leant over to gaze into the flowing depths. Swirling colors were what she saw at first, and then, as her vision became more focused, she observed, where her own reflection should have been, a gnarled old tree with a gaping red mouth, stretching its branches toward her.

Evelyn leapt back from the water's edge, and then crept near again for another look. This time all she could see in the water was the waving of the half-submerged plants, whose leaves thrived in the water as well as on land. She looked about her at the solemn congress of trees, grateful for their protection. She knew they would take care of her.

Evelyn reached her cottage, just as the sun had exhausted its prerogatives. She selected a bottle of wine from the refrigerator and poured a goblet, which she placed, with Thoreau, on a table next to a comfortable chair, intending to finish the book before dinner. Before she sat down, there was a knock at the door.

"Well met, Evelyn," was the salutation she received from the tall woman attired in a sophisticated suit of raven black hue when she opened her door. It was Elizabeth Darkner, the owner of the Top of the World. Absently tucking her long, blonde hair behind her ear, Elizabeth bade her, "Please step outside, my dear. I have come to speak with you."

"Of course, Ms. Darkner. Hello," stammered Evelyn, ill at ease as she went out of the warm cottage into the stygian night. "I am surprised to see you here."

Elizabeth touched her long, delicate fingers to Evelyn's forearm and exerted a slight pressure with her red-lacquered nails, indenting Evelyn's skin with five miniature crescents. "We at the lodge are aware of your devotion to Black Mountain."

"Oh, yes, Ma'am, I love the trees."

"That is precisely the reason for our visit."

"Our?" asked Evelyn, looking around nervously, seeing only the shades between the trees and the branches swaying in the cool breeze, barely discernible in the negligible light of the moon veiled by the trees.

"You, of all people, dear, should understand," issued from the red lips of her employer, as, from behind her, Evelyn felt her arms being seized. "The mountain must have blood."

"No!" screamed Evelyn, as black-cloaked figures pulled her into the wood. They held her to the trunk of the same eldritch tree that she had venerated that very morning, stretching her arms behind her and binding them to the thick circumference of the trunk. As she fought against her captors, the bark of the tree tore at her clothing and serrated her back and elbows. Evelyn heard the sighs of the wind mingling with her screams.

Pale in the cadaverous moonlight, the high priestess assumed her place before the sacrificial victim, and she spread her arms—which had become feathered wings—and received the ritual blade from a cowled disciple.

"This is the altar of the Great Unseen. It shall be fertilized with the blood of its handmaiden. The mountain must be fed."

"No! I loved you so!" cried Evelyn to the laughing trees, as the branches moved to enclose her in a final caress.

Carter wondered who wrote these awful stories. Were they works of fiction—or fact? And, if fact, who was the author's informant? Obviously, Evelyn could not have told her horrible story to a biographer. This Elizabeth Darkner—she seemed to be the ringleader. If Dr. Campbell was still alive and active, he should have got the lady's story by now. Unless the feds didn't consider the professor entitled to classified information (they were like that). He wondered if he should check into the hotel when he got to the top of the mountain.

There were still three or four hours of daylight remaining, so Carter continued upward, wishing to see as much of the mountain as he could before bedding down for the night. Nearly an hour elapsed before he came upon an interesting arrangement of oblong stones in a tiny clearing, an open space on a rocky ledge overlooking the forest below. It was a dizzyingly steep drop from the ledge to the tops of the pines in the valley.

The stones were set into the rock, so as to stand as if they were playing cards fixed in an upright position. He quickly looked around, to make certain he was not being observed, and then he left the cover afforded by the trees to study the stones. Each monolith was embellished with a single relief—a bird, a mountain, a pentacle, a skull—the motifs of the cave reiterated on the stones. Carter retreated into the wood and began sketching and making notes in his book. Before he resumed his explorations, he just had to read one more file.

Virgin Wood

"How'd it happen, Sheriff?" The reporter was looking intently at the tarp that was covering two lumps on a patch of blood-gored ground.

"All we know at this time is that some back-to-nature types were backpacking through the woods near the bottom of Black Mountain and were alarmed by an odor—a stink. Upon investigation they uncovered a young couple who had been sliced into shreds, their remains strewn halfway between their tent and the campfire. The hikers called 911, and law enforcement responded and are currently on the scene."

"Who were they?"

"The victims have not been identified yet. Forensics is en route from Portsmouth; they'll probably I.D. them."

"Any idea who could have done this?" the television reporter from Portsmouth asked.

"No further comment at this time."

"There you have it," to the cameraman, "the third unexplained murder in Putnam County this month. What evil is walking in such idyllic landscape? Keep tuned to this station. We will bring you updates as we receive them."

"The generator is fully operational now," John said as he high-fived his wife. "I knew I could figure it out. You're married to a genius."

Ann beamed at him. "You have always had a knack for fixing things."

"Well, if a guy's going to retire with his beloved wife to a log cabin in the middle of nowhere, he'd best possess at least a modicum of mechanical aptitude. By the way, I have just remembered something: this Wednesday, when we make our monthly trek into Portsmouth to get provisions and new books from the library—that's the day the travel writer will be speaking at the library. Perhaps we can catch her talk while we're in town."

"Sounds good to me." Amy placed her arms around him and squeezed him tight, her eyes wide. "Just think, John: we are, as far as I can tell, *the first humans* to make a home on this particular parcel of real estate. I'm so glad we used our own trees for the timber: our cabin has grown out from the wood and remains a part of it. Now, dear, please indulge me with a handsome pose. I would like to take a photo of you by the door of the cabin—to commemorate the sixth-month anniversary of our life on the mountain."

"Yes, my love. Has it really been six months already? Six months of glorious liberty in the maternal bosom of nature. I'm sure I would prefer never to don a suit and tie again—except, of course, when I take my gal out on the town. How would you feel about celebrating our fortieth anniversary at the Top of the World?"

"Oh, John, that would be splendid! The Top of the World is a *very* exclusive lodge at the top of our mountain. That should be a great treat. Shall we go inside now and eat our dinner? Would you like to read Dostoevsky tonight?"

"This horrible blizzard seems to have blown in from out of nowhere, John. How much snow do you think we'll get? Do you think we will be snowed in?"

"We'll be just fine. We have to get used to nor'easters, now that we'll be living here. I have already performed routine maintenance on the snow blower and the plow—and both are in good working order. We needn't resort to cannibalism to survive, because our pantry is well stocked with nonperishables, and we have laid by a great supply of wood for the stove. If worse comes to worst, we can keep each other warm under the blankets until spring."

"Retirement hasn't cooled *your* engines any, dear. Let me go, honey. I have to get the hotcakes off the stove."

"I can't sleep—those branches are striking the roof pretty hard. I'm concerned about damage to the shingles and the roof."

"Ann, there can be no question of branches being close enough to touch our roof. Surely you must remember how, when we were landscaping the yard and garden, we removed all the trees in the vicinity of the house; in fact, we designed the landscaping with the intent of ensuring adequate clearance, so that no trees could ever fall on the house. Don't allow the storm to frighten you so."

"Nonetheless, I am positive that the noise on the roof is the sound of branches hitting the roof. I'll get my coat and boots and take a look."

"I'm coming, too—

"Look! *Look!* There are *two trees in the yard!*—to the right of the door. They weren't there this morning. They weren't! *We cut them all down,* Ann—they weren't there! *We cut them all down! We cut them all down!*"

"I know, John. I know. *Oh, God—what is happening? How can the trees be there, when we cut them down?* We must go back inside at once—we'll get frostbite."

"Here, you're covered with snow. Take off that coat. That—that—branch— It *really is* a branch—it's hitting the window. How—?"

"Help me nail this picture up over the glass. Here we go. Now, let's move the dresser in front of it."

"John! John!—a branch crashed through the other

window—there is glass all over the kitchen. *What is happening, John?"* The crackling of splintering timber preceded the emergence of a great root through the floorboards. Ann leapt to the side of the room.

"Ann, get your coat—we've got to get to the car. Where are the damn keys? Out—get out! Now!" A huge, gnarly limb crashed through the ceiling.

"John—the car—there's a tree on top of it!"

"Let's go on foot. Come—let's get moving! Hurry, Ann.— Who are you, Bud? What's the big idea?"

"Stop it! He didn't do anything! Leave him alone! Ugghh!"

"Sheriff Johnston, where is the old man?"

"Dead, High Priestess."

"Very well. Cut the carcass into pieces and hang them from the trees. Bring the woman."

"Who *are* you, lady? Just what are you doing here? Where is my husband?"

"Oh!" as her jaw cracked when Johnston threw his fist. She crumpled, and he pulled her back to her feet. She looked up as the woman with long blonde hair lifted her arms—which were now black-feathered wings—and, though her mouth was filled with blood, she screamed, as the bird-woman spake:

"With this dagger Black Mountain shall be avenged—with the woman's tongue shall the winged beasts feed their young in their nests, and her blood shall fertilize the altar—for the virgin wood has been defiled—the eldritch trees disemboweled and dismembered—the altar profaned."

"Blood. The mountain must have blood," chanted the dozen black-cowled figures emerging from the woods, carrying boughs of fir trees high above their heads.

"Snow run hot, run red with blood. With red blood we shall fertilize the altar of the Great Unseen. The mountain must be fed. The mountain must have blood."

"Sheriff Johnston, any word on the retired couple who disappeared? Their kids are frantic. Their car was smashed by a fallen tree—like a pancake—and the log cabin looks as if it has been through a hurricane: there are tree roots coming up through the floor, and branches through the roof."

"The investigation is ongoing. We'll keep you updated, Bill."

"Stay tuned to Portsmouth television for continuing coverage of breaking news. For the very latest updates, you can go to our website and click on Putnam County Murders."

Those poor backpackers—he recalled hearing something about the unlucky kids in the news a few years back. He'd have to dig into the TV station's archives, see if he could locate the reporter. The Putnam County Murders stories were what had caught his attention in the first place. Carter had been investigating the shady Putnam County finances about that time—had not made any friends in the county offices, he was certain. Yes, he'd better take his finding to Boston.

Daylight was waning, so he got moving again. He'd wait until he found a place to camp for the night before he ate again.

He was also feeling the danger closing in on him.

When he took a brief break from hiking to drink some water and to ease the cramps in his legs, Carter pulled out the next file, "Susan and Eben." Hidden under a pine tree with a thirty-foot spread at the base, he pulled out his light and began reading.

Old Jim Brantley's Cabin

The Brantley house was where it had always been, ever since Jim Brantley felled some trees and split enough logs to build it. It had smelt of death, even at the onset. Jim split the skulls of his wife, Elspeth, and the boy, too, figuring he might as well, as long as he was chopping anyway. The house had been in the same spot, in the shadow of Black Mountain—stayed put even when the natives Old Jim had displaced by settling there took to throwing tomahawks as a kind of eviction notice. In the end they scalped Brantley but left his cabin be. The grass hadn't grown too high before some trappers squatted there for the winter, always bringing half-dead critters in and cutting the skins off 'em.

The house wasn't figuring on going anywhere. Got kind of used to the blood soaking its floors from time to time. Kept them from drying out.

Time to time, kids'd come across the cabin as they hunted birds or berries in the woods. Sometimes they never went out of the woods again. No one ever thought to look under the floor boards.

Yes, the house liked it right where it was. It was a house of habit. It had got used to things.

In the 1690s the house saw an increase in traffic through the wilderness. After half of Salem had been jailed or hanged, people were moving out of the Massachusetts colony, some of them refugeeing up north to Black Mountain. Some of the Putnams considered it would be best if they moved on, too, quick-like.

Some time ago a family in a big wagon piled high with furniture and trunks and pulled by a team of mules found the deserted cabin. They built a large frame house right next to the old cabin, intended to use the older house as a dairy. The woman hung sheets and coveralls on a clothesline and sent her children into the woods to forage for berries to fill her pies. One day the children did not come home for dinner and the woman had to go looking for them.

"Daniel, Martha! Where are you? It's time to get home for dinner. Stew's ready! Papa will be waiting for us," she called and called, out of patience. She found them climbing on a pile of rocks, their berry baskets on the ground a little way off. The forest was filled with strange cairns and compositions of large rocks laid out in unnatural patterns by unnamed hands. Folk said they were arranged to complement the stars and the planets, sun and moon. Most people avoided the rocky forest, especially at the solstices and equinoxes, for it was felt to house something evil—impalpable and evil. "You know better than to play on the stones!"

She had to pull them down from the cairn and drag them by their ears to their baskets; and as she did so, she tried not to look at the strange carvings on the stones: squares and circles, stars, weird animals. With clammy palms she pushed her children before her, herded them home.

Her thoughts divided between her children's weird behavior and the stew burning in the hearth, she bundled the children into the house, calling, "Peter, we're home!" When her husband did not answer, she ordered the boy and girl to stay in the house while she looked around in back.

Peter was hanging from an apple tree, his feet in a noose, and his blood running from the jagged gashes in his throat to sate the thirsty earth.

Leaving everything behind, Pearl put the children in the cart, hitched the mules, and drove all day along the rough trail, which was more holes than road, followed the river to the tiny settlement of lean-to shacks and tents at the base of Black Mountain. The tavernkeeper put them in a room in the back; later he arranged for their possessions to be carted from the house in the woods. Pearl, from that time, was an idiot, and the children grew up wild, living mostly in the forest.

The house waited uncomplainingly, enjoying the tickling of rodent feet running between the floorboards and the logs of the walls, and the flutter of wings in the attic, where the black birds built their nests. Triangular grey-spotted spiders were busy at their spinning, and spindly-legged black ants were gnawing sawdust out of lumber. Relentless spring rains and winter snowstorms had caused the walls to slump over time and the door to droop on its hinges. Gales repeatedly came in from over the ocean, taking some of the shingles with them when they left and providing the raindrops an ingress into the upper story and a nursery for several species of fungi, so that the beams grew soft and the house had the aroma of a crypt.

One day the house knew that new people were moving in. It shuddered and creaked in contemplation of their imminent arrival. The lopsided door swung open.

"Here. We can stay here, Sue. No one will find us so deep in the woods."

Eben stopped the horses and helped his sweetheart down. Gathering her in his arms, he gave her a long kiss on the lips, after which he gingerly patted her belly.

"You're not going to hurt the baby, dear," she smiled at him. "So we're to set up housekeeping here?"

"It's a nice house, Susan, needing only some repairs, I think. Let's look it over."

Thirty minutes later they were unloading their satchels and bedrolls from the horses.

"No one knows us in New Hampshire, so it's a good place to start a new life. As God is my witness, as soon as it is safe I will make you my wife. But Lord knows your father will kill the both of us if he finds out. Tomorrow, while you try to clean as best you can with water from the river and make the house our home, I'm going to run out for some provisions and tools. There's bound to be someone set up for trading further upriver."

Thus, Susan and Eben commenced housekeeping together, avoiding society, living off the land.

Eben had just joined his regiment in New York when he had received a letter from Susan, telling him she was with child and that she had been thrown out of her home by her father. An outcast, she wrote that she was hiding in the hayloft in the barn of her best friend's farm. Eben had no choice but to desert the Union Army and take two horses with him. Some friends surreptitiously helped him, but being a fugitive, he was reluctant to involve his family in his trouble. Eben patched and repaired the house and Susan cooked good meals in the hearth, so that the dampness of the house was somewhat mitigated. They bought a cow and housed her in the old log cabin with the horses. In six months' time Eben had become a good hunter and Susan a good forager; and she had planted a garden next to the house. It was fruitful, but the plants were small and sickly-appearing.

"I'm so glad to have the garden now. Mostly because I no longer have to go into the woods for herbs and berries as much. The woods don't feel godly, Eben."

Their sleep had been diminished many a night by the woodland animals' conversations in the dark and the wind's rattling the trees awake from their slumbers. Howls and low growls and murmurs, occasional scratches at the wooden walls by some unseen animal, and the moan of the wind as it entered the caves and hollows of the mountain and blew through the trees' branches—these were their evensong.

"You can stay here, Susan, while I check the traps tomorrow. No sense in both of us going in the woods."

The next day was sunny and warm for late October, so Susan put off her chores to walk with her lover into the woods, which did not seem as forbidding on a bright day. At first it was pleasant to walk beneath the trees, and they picked nosegays of forest blossoms together; but, as they walked deeper into the forest, the curtain of leaves began to obscure the sunlight, and the damp earth exhaled coldness into the air. Susan would not have questioned Eben, but he himself volunteered his frustration at not being able to find the traps: he always kept them in the same places, he said, but they must have made a wrong turn, for they had already been walking for an hour. She agreed when Eben said they should go back home and try again the next day to find the traps, but really she was afraid that they were altogether lost and that getting home might not be so easy. She cradled her increasing belly in both hands as they began to walk back to the house.

"I've got to rest a minute, dear," Susan softly announced thirty minutes later, as she lowered herself onto a boulder.

Eben sat beside her and looked around worriedly: trees, lots of trees, decreasing daylight, treacherously slick and muddy clay earth. Why had he not marked his path to the traps? Why had he allowed Susan to come with him? Heaping recriminations upon himself, his eyes cast down, he started—drew his hands back from the stone on which they were sitting, for he had noticed strange markings on the stones. Unnerved, he looked at Susan, saw the fatigue in her eyes, and then looked down again at the stone. Circles, stars, strange beasts: these, along with the letters of some strange, inhuman alphabet, had been carved into the rock with a knife. Who had done it?

He turned his head to look behind—and glimpsed a cairn, a pyramidal pile of large stones, glowing orange in the dappled light of the setting sun.

"Susan, honey, can you walk some more now? We should get home before it gets dark."

She said that she was ready and apologized for the delay. They resumed walking.

"Eben, look!" She pointed to a tree on which were painted two triangles, positioned to suggest a pair of red wings.

"Let's go, Susan," Eben said, urging her forward.

"Sorry, Eben," Susan apologized, vanishing into the brush. A late-pregnant woman, she had the need to empty her bladder more than was convenient.

"Oh, let's get going!" In a tone of urgency she spurred him on when she had finished. Her face was white, and she was trembling. Clutching her abdomen, she repeated, "Let's get going."

Out of view, behind the brush, she had spied a ten-foot-long stone slab, raised like a table-top upon two piles of rocks. The slab was deeply stained—impregnated with a rusty reddish, blood-like stain—and on top of it lay the bones of a human finger, knuckle joints. Not waiting for Eben's reply, she walked faster, scanning the forest floor for the vines and roots that lay in wait for opportunities to trip people and prevent them from leaving the woods.

When, with relief, they thought that they were nearing the house, Susan disappeared abruptly into the foliage, crying "Help! *Eben, help!*"

Screaming, *"Susan!"* Eben ran after her—ran through cattails and brambles that lacerated his clothing and skin until he found himself grappling with two men with powerful arms. As he struggled to free himself, he noticed that his captors were wearing black, hooded cloaks. He saw that their hands were dark with tattoos in the style of the engravings on the stones.

"*Let me go!* What do you want?" he screamed at them. "I've got to help my wife!"

"The mountain must have blood," one of his captors spoke.

"The mountain must have blood," the other repeated.

Eben desperately fought the abductors as they pulled him toward a clearing, where Susan was already stretched out upon the sodden forest floor, held in place by the black-robed figures who were fastening her hands and feet to stakes set in the ground. In the struggle, the hood was pushed back from the savage visage of one of the men—

"Putnam! What in God's name are you doing, George Putnam?" cried Eben.

"In *God's name*—the *mountain* god's name—we are fertilizing the altar. The mountain must have blood."

The assembled cultists repeated the refrain: "The mountain must have blood. Blood unto the mountain."

Eben's knees gave out.

Susan screamed as they cut his throat and gloated over the red froth coursing into the earth.

Sobbing hysterically—*for Eben was dead*—she did not see the approach of the hooded figure who was holding a dagger over her stomach.

"Not my baby!" she cried when the cultist raised her arm above her abdomen.

When it was done, the bloody babe was placed in a basket upon the stone slab, slick with its mother's entrails.

A great hawk swooped suddenly from the wickerwork of branches above, took up the basket in its claws, and flew away with it beyond the treetops, to the top of the mountain, where the caves glow crimson on the Autumn Equinox and emit sonorous sighs.

At the bottom of Black Mountain the old house was replete.

The tone of this narration was a bit too playful for his tastes—God, it described the ritual murders of innocent people, as if it were telling a ghost story around a campfire! This writer was some kind of sicko. The other stories—they felt a little too real for ghost stories, too.

He had to face facts: he had gotten in over his head. This was not the storm-tossed Atlantic with a mysterious triangle in which ill-fated vessels disappeared over the ocean, lost to the briny depths. Neither was this a small desert town populated with UFOlogists. This was a place where sicko people preyed upon unwary interlopers. A mountain harboring serial killers.

Carter dismissed the stories of ladies turning into birds, possessed farms and houses, and a living godlike mountain. Obviously these

126

were fables with which to manipulate a cult full of naïve devotees and gullible idiots. He read the next file.

Black Mountain Travel & Tourism

"Oh, darn!" Alexandra depressed the brake pedal, letting her car coast across the lane to the shoulder, where she placed it in park. She got out and walked all around the car, looking at its underside from all angles. *I wonder what the crunching sound was,* she thought. She could see nothing broken or hanging, and the tires weren't flat. *It must be just the ruts and rocks on this rough road.* She got back in the car.

Alexandra had been motoring up the winding two-lane highway, by means of which she would be exploring New Hampshire, driving from the bottom to the top of it. The first part of the day she had spent wandering around strange stone formations, reputed to be the work of the ancient Atlantic-traversing Celts, tucked deep within the primeval forest of the southern part of the state; she felt this attraction would provide material for a chapter in her work-in-progress, *Road Trips of New England: Hidden Gems.* She had examined the enigmatic arrangement of stones that were aligned with the celestial motions, as well as the mysterious speaking tube that could enable a person to throw his voice, causing it to appear to originate from somewhere else. Many people considered the curious placement of the great rocks and boulders a hefty sort of practical joke, she knew, but she intended to interview the locals for their take on the phenomenon.

As she continued northward from the Massachusetts border, toward the craggy, snow-topped mountainous terrain of New

Hampshire, she found the road becoming narrower and the exits spaced further apart. She could see nothing to the left—nor to the right—of the road, except for the crystal-clear water that was streaming downhill from the snowy mountain in pebble-strewn creek beds, beyond which a wall of thick woods disallowed further sight. Before and behind her she saw only the yellow-striped black pavement—as far as the next curve in the road. She pulled over and rolled her window down, lifted her camera from the empty passenger seat, and snapped photos of a sign with an arrow that pointed to a tree-darkened dirt road branching from the highway on the left. The hand-lettered sign boasted: *Bide-a-While Inn, the Best Food in These Parts. Forsaken, New Hampshire. Pop. ~~78~~ 77.*

Alexandra backed her car up on the pothole-infested road and made a left turn. "Better take the opportunity to interview some locals about the stones. This sign— Whoa! Great cover art for my book." Her car lumped down the bumpy road to the Bide-a-While. She looked at her watch and saw that it was two o'clock: "If I stay no more than an hour, I believe I can still make it to the Top of the World, my hotel on the top of Black Mountain, before dark."

Fifteen vertebrae-smashing, bumpy minutes later, she arrived at a clearing in the woods. She passed six or seven trailers, a couple of weathered log cabins, an unmarked dirt road on the left, and two more trailers, whose awnings were either hanging limply or lying upon the ground. Several scruffy hounds pulled at their chains as they strained to get at her car.

She slammed on the brakes—a deer sped across her path. She was thinking that maybe this was not a good idea . . . Forsaken was not all that picturesque a hamlet, after all. Perhaps she should go back. But where could she turn around? She'd have to pull into someone's yard to do that, or that narrow road that had no sign, and neither alterative was appealing. Just then she saw some lights—a neon sign designating a brown frame building with a screen door that was propped open: Bide-a-While Inn.

"Well, I'm here. Might as well get it over." Alexandra pulled up to the inn and parked next to the door. She reached for her purse and her notebook and pen, locked the car, and ventured inside.

"Hello," she called to the empty counter, lined with ripped red barstools on chrome bases that had seen better days. "Anyone here?"

"Oh, my, oh, my, well, what do we have here?" the question preceded the speaker through the swinging pair of louvered doors. And then a woman in a garish dress with a loud geranium print and dirty sneakers without shoelaces emerged. "Hi, miss. What can I do for you?"

"Good afternoon. I'm looking for a cup of coffee and someone to talk to about this part of New Hampshire. I'm writing a travel guide."

"Bless your heart, miss, here, take a seat, I'll start the coffee. Are you traveling alone? Where are you headed?" She clattered the chipped china and filled the coffee carafe with water.

"I'm on my way to the lodge on top of Black Mountain. I believe it's only a few miles up the main road."

"It sure is. It sure is. Here's a napkin and some cream and sugar. You'll be there in no time at all. What did you want to ask about the area, miss?"

"Well, I visited the strange stones, down by the New Hampshire border, this morning. May I start there? What do you think of them?"

"Well, miss, them's downright eldritch stones . . . from the ancient people of Europe. They came here to claim the land for their ancient gods and curious ways. That's what I always heard. Could be just an old legend, though. How's a person to know?"

"Have you ever visited there?"

"Oh, once, a long time ago. People hereabouts usually stay away. Tourists like to stop there and take pictures and talk about hoaxes and pulling one over on out-of-towners and such."

"Have you lived here all your life?"

"Yes, miss, I grew up right here, at the bottom of Black Mountain. My dad and mum, and me and my husband have always run the diner and the store. Coffee's ready. Here you go, nice and hot."

"Seventy-seven people live here, according to the sign."

"Yes, miss. Anthony—that was my husband—died a couple of weeks ago, bringing us down to seventy-seven. He accidentally cut off his hand with an axe and bled to death. Nobody found him until it was too late."

"Oh, you poor woman. My condolences on the loss of your husband. The coffee was wonderful. Here's ten dollars—keep the change. Consider it a fair payment for a delightful conversation, helping me to learn about Forsaken. Oh, by the way, how'd this little town get that name?"

"That's what the last minister said as he hightailed it out of here in his horse-cart. He didn't make it very far before a tree fell on him and crushed both him and his horse. Waste of a good horse, if you ask me. 'God has forsaken you heathens!' he screamed."

"On that interesting note of history, I'll say thank you and goodbye. I've got a dinner reservation at the lodge on Black Mountain this evening. It has been a pleasure meeting you. Mighty good coffee, Mrs. . . . ?" and she extended her hand.

"The mountain must have blood!" the woman said as she snapped a handcuff on Alexandra's wrist. "The mountain must be fed."

"Lady—just what in the hell do you think you're doing!" Alexandra pulled her arm away.

"Hey, Ma, give me. I'll take her to the altar." Alexandra spun to see the two men who were blocking the doorway.

"Okay, James. You and Jesse take her. Wait—give me her keys. I want to move her car."

The woman reached behind the filthy counter and withdrew a black robe, which she slid over her head. She pulled out two more and handed one to each of the boys, who put them on, and they all exited the Bide-a-While, pulling a kicking and screaming Alexandra with them.

Seventy-four black-hooded people awaited them out on the rutted dirt road. "Blood, the mountain must have blood," they chanted.

Alexandra tried to pull away, but Jesse had fastened the handcuff to his belt. As she struggled, a child—or a child-sized, black-robed ghoul—kicked her ankles and knocked her to the ground.

Her arm still handcuffed to Jesse's belt, the crowd dragged her down the unmarked road. Her exposed flesh was raw and bloody by the time they reached the derelict farm at the end of the road, which appeared to have been abandoned many years.

"Officer Johnston," called the woman that James and Jesse had addressed as *Ma*. "Officer, you got a key for this cuff?"

"Howdy, Ma'am, nice to see you again. Nice day. Who's the chickadee?"

"Writer—stopped in for an *interview*. She's gonna see the sights tonight."

"Altar's ready for the sacrifice. The high priestess is on her way from the lodge."

A shiny black Land Rover pulled into the barnyard, and a tall, woman with hair of spun gold emerged from it. Her full red lips parted, and she said softly, "Let us begin."

As Johnston unlocked the handcuff, Alexandra attempted once more to break free—but she was immediately overpowered by the mob. Cowled figures held her writhing body down on the dry dirt. Alexandra tried to bite Jesse's hand as he tied a rope around each of her wrists and ankles, which another hooded monster fastened to the ground with stakes.

As the black-clad coven formed a circle around her, Alexandra screamed to a relentless, aloof universe.

The high priestess intoned:

"Bleed her blood into the ground.

The gods of old, the gods from the time before Man.

The gods from the time before the Black Mountain.

The gods from before the earth.
The gods crave blood.
Fertilize the altar with her blood.
This woman desired knowledge, which she shall have.
The mountain must be fed.
The mountain must have blood."

Carter groaned—vomited. He knew Alexandra: they had worked together in a small Boston-area weekly newspaper. He had passed the Bide-a-While Inn sign when he drove up the mountain. Is this what happened to my missing colleague? He moaned, clutching his abdomen, tears streaming from his eyes. Is this what happened to them all?

He had to read the rest of the files: daylight was fast running out. He would camp beneath the concealing shelter of the centuries-old tree, perhaps the safest hideout he could find, anyway. One by one he read, with increasing anguish, "Mr. and Mrs. Randolph and Anne Sanderson," "E. A. Darkner," "Joanna and Danielle."

Black Mountain Get-Away

"This romantic property is the perfect escape from the stresses of everyday life. Briarton Manor is a chic bed-and-breakfast snuggled into the side of the forested Black Mountain in the northern reaches of New Hampshire. Find solace in Nature while being pampered with fresh-cooked breakfasts and champagne brunches beneath the spreading pines. Call our toll-free number to reserve your luxury vacation."

Randolph folded up the *Wall Street Journal*. When his wife, Anne, returned to the breakfast table with a second cup of hot caramel coffee, he said, "So we're agreed? I'll ask my secretary to make our reservation today, and Friday morning we can drive up to the mountain."

"Yes, Randy, we can use a vacation. The inn sounds very lovely," Anne replied.

A few days later they were headed north. The rush-hour traffic at the southern end of New Hampshire waned quickly as they motored toward the mountains. By mid-morning four lanes had become two, and cars had become only occasional. The sky was hardly visible now—the inclining road before, the tall trees on both sides of the road, and the snaking road behind making a concerted effort to prohibit most views beyond the slender highway. Likewise, the forest and streams were strenuously pressing themselves against the pavement, as if they would retard the incursion of civilization. The forensic evidence of a natural malice was damning, for the mountain had strewn the decaying trunks of its trees haphazardly along the shoulder of the road, and it had tossed barren branches into the path of the vehicles. Accidents, most likely, were not accidental.

The Sandersons, caught up by the beauty of nature, were blind to these intimations of malevolence. The couple were relishing the start of a week away from the cares of earning a living, balancing bank accounts, and winterizing their home. Wrapped in their daydreams, they failed to notice the downward slide of the sun, nor did they attend to the flocks of crows that were swooping back and forth across the road, daring death as they lunged between tangled branches as acrobats do on trapezes.

It was late autumn: the days were short, and the nights were long. By mid-afternoon the sun had dipped below the tree line, concealing itself from the shadows until it could come out of hiding in the morning.

"How much farther, Randy?" asked Anne, noting nervously that the unlit road was bereft of travelers, except for themselves.

"We should be close. Keep an eye out for a sign for Briarton Manor, or for Gristle Lane. If you see a gas station, speak up. We should fill the tank at the next opportunity."

"It's kind of lonely up here, isn't it?" said Anne. "What kind of name is Gristle Lane?"

Randolph swerved the car—squealed the tires—slammed on the brakes. On only two wheels, their car skidded, sideswiping a prodigious tree with a great groaning of metal.

"Are you all right, Anne?" he cried. "Oh, God, I'm so sorry. I'm so sorry, Anne. Are you all right?"

"I'm fine, Randy, just shaken. What happened?" she said, trying to stop her trembling.

"That—that thing—that thing ran across the road! Did you see it?" She had not. "It was big as a man—bigger—but it was running on all fours. In the sunset, with the light in my eyes, I couldn't see it clearly. I suppose I over-corrected—but, honey, I don't know what it was that ran in front of us! It was . . . unearthly!"

"We'd better take a look at the damage to the car," Anne suggested. They both exited the car from the driver's side door; Anne's door had been jammed shut. The rear tire being flat, Randolph attempted to summon roadside assistance on his cell phone, but they had no service this far into the wilderness. He opened the trunk and removed his jack, knowing that he had to hurry—he was not an expert at changing tires, and it was fast becoming dark.

"Honey, come here," he said. His wife came to his side. "Anne, I think something is watching us from the woods. Keep an eye out, please—and keep your hand on the car door, so that you can jump in fast if you need to."

"What is it?" she whispered, bending low to his ear as he sought his tools in the trunk. "I feel it, too."

"Oh, we should have been at the inn by now—if only I hadn't been so stupid! It's all my fault. I'll fix this, dear, and we'll be all right."

He blamed himself as he pulled the tire iron from the trunk. Hearing a rustling in the woods, they both turned their heads in the direction of the sound—but the woods were now much too dark to see into. Randolph fitted the iron onto the nuts, trying to work as quickly as he could. The rustling became more continuous, sounding like someone—or something—pacing through the leaves. Anne scanned the dense arrangement of tree trunks, seeking the source of the crackling and shuffling sounds, maintaining her hold of the driver's side door, ready to pull it open in an instant if it were necessary to get inside fast. She thought she heard a snuffling or snorting kind of sound, like that of a dog or a horse, but she did not remark upon it, fearing to distract her husband from his work.

"I can't get this damn nut loose! I don't know if it's rusted or if the wheel's bent," Randolph fumed. It was getting darker.

Headlights appeared in the distance—coming from up the mountain, from the direction in which they were headed.

"Randy, a car is coming. They can help us," Anne said.

Her husband knew better, though. A preternatural instinct was gripping him in the head, the chest, and the groin—it was holding him fast, burning his blood, and making him breathe hard. He seized his wife's hand and said, "*Run! This way!*"

They fled into the forest, running in the opposite direction from the source of the rustling sounds. It was shadowy beneath the canopy of leaves. The sun, now too low upon the horizon, could not shine in the woods. The man and wife did not know where they were going, but they kept going, trying to avoid falling over the roots and running into the low branches. But the twisted vegetation reached toward them, curled around Randolph's ankle, and pulled him down. Anne turned to assist him to his feet.

She ran straight into a black-robed man—a tall, hefty man, whose head was covered by a cowl, and whose face was indistinguishable in the darkness.

"Please help—my husband . . ." Her voice trailed off, for the man was not responding to her plea. He stood between herself and Randolph. "Let me by—I need to—" He stretched his arm to prevent her from going around him to her husband.

"I will help you," he said. "You are expected at Briarton Manor, are you not? We became concerned, and so we came to find you."

"Oh, I see, oh, yes—I mean, thank you. We had an accident, you see—a flat tire. My husband—"

"We have attended to him already." He took her elbow—she tried to take her arm back—but the man held it firmly in his grip, guiding her back to the road. A great beast sprang past them—it galloped across the road, ran into the forest on the other side of the road. Then three more black robed and hooded people arrived—encircled Randolph.

"Randy, what's going on?" she asked.

The great beast—a wolf, twice as large as a man—cantered back across the road. It paced around the car. It walked in circles around the six people who were standing in the road. Anne stifled her screams, knowing that screaming would only draw the animal's attention.

Two of the men bound her wrists. Two more bound her husband's hands. The beast continued to snarl and pace. A tall, blonde woman emerged from the dark forest.

"The mountain must have blood," she said through her gorgeous, ruby-red lips. She lifted her arms—they were black-feathered wings, not human appendages.

"High Priestess, the mountain must be fed," said the man who had dragged Anne out of the woods.

The four robed men had formed a circle around Randolph and Anne; but when the priestess drew nigh they withdrew into the wood, leaving the couple alone on the road with her. The great wolf walked all around Randolph and Anne, sniffing their bodies.

"The mountain must have blood. Hot, red blood shall fertilize the altar of the Great Unseen," spake the priestess.

"The mountain must have blood," echoed the congregants with one voice in a damned refrain.

Randolph stared in fear as the wolf approached him. Anne sobbed.

"Blood unto the mountain. Red runs the streams. The mountain will have blood," the cowled group intoned, as the wolf tore them apart.

Carter seized the next file.

The Lady of the Mountain

"Don't worry so—she's a beautiful, healthy baby," said Marilyn. "Elizabeth Angelique Darkner. Our little angel."

"Undeniably, our little girl is the most striking infant I have ever seen (not that I pay a lot of attention to babies). But why is her hair blonde, Marilyn? And her eyes—so large, so *blue!* Look at those dark eyelashes," wondered Daniel. "We are both brunette and brown-eyed."

He did not notice that his wife averted her face.

She was thinking of the dream—but had it been a dream? Nine months before their daughter was born—it had been their first Halloween—and she and Daniel had returned to their penthouse at the Top of the World, their luxury lodge on the summit of Black Mountain, following a costume ball which they had held in celebration of the successful first year of their venture, after which, they had helped each other with the removal of their vampire costumes. With much congratulatory and flirtatious banter all mixed up together, they had unlaced, unzipped, and flung away bodices and capes. They had made love as they had not since their wedding night—they had been virgins then, with an eternity of stored-up lovemaking to expend. In their shared triumph, they had detonated in passion.

Awakened by a noise on the balcony, Marilyn had glimpsed a shadowy form behind the sheer curtains; had slid out from beneath her sleeping husband's hairy arm; had tiptoed toward the glass doors, pausing halfway between the bed and the curtains. She could still recall hearing strange notes—a weird night music which seemed to come on the wind—remembered moving toward the French doors, caught up by the beguiling melody, and coming to a man waiting on the other side. Crossing the plush silver carpet, she had drawn open the doors in a single captivating choreography. The tall, dark man on the balcony had opened his arms, and she had stepped, unclothed, into them. He had made love to her as no mortal man could. Staring into his red, blazing eyes, she had not felt the cold—still, as he had moved his lips behind her ear, she had shivered. She had shivered, too, when he pierced her skin with his teeth and drank of her.

She vividly remembered waking from her dream—and recalled her surprise at finding that she had sleepwalked naked onto the balcony and into the swirling snow. She recalled looking to the bed; remembered seeing that Daniel was still deep in slumber; remembered quietly slipping into the bed beside him. She had never told anyone of that dream.

"Marilyn, earth to Marilyn," Daniel prodded her. "What are you thinking about so intensely?"

"Oh, nothing I'm just tired," she answered. She bent down to the pink-ribboned bassinet to kiss her darling—and drew back, screaming.

"Honey—*Oh God*!" Daniel said, picking up a powder-blue bath blanket to arrest the flow of blood from Marilyn's cheek, where the baby had sliced a crevice from her earlobe to the corner of her mouth. As he helped his wife to the bathroom, Daniel glanced at his newborn daughter in her blood-spattered bassinet—the nail of the infant Elizabeth's left forefinger was as curved and as sharp as a talon and red with her mother's blood!

Over the next two decades, Elizabeth had matured in pulchritude, poise, and intellect, studying business law in Salem; and, during breaks from her coursework, she had provided considerable assistance to her parents in the management of the Top of the

World. Daniel and Marilyn had always felt an unnamable reserve, a weird barrier between themselves and their child, and yet they adored her. Having taken her degree, Elizabeth was to come home now, for good. For months her parents had been preparing for her return, and a mountain of boxes, wrapped in ice blue tissue and silver foil, awaited her in her suite.

At noon, an ocean-blue Ferrari crested the twisted road of the mountain, safely delivering Elizabeth to her ancestral manor. A dozen crimson-coated bellmen were arrayed in formation on either side of the brass and glass front doors of the Top of the World and the concierge was waiting on the red carpet when the Ferrari glided up to the door.

When Elizabeth had been properly welcomed by the staff, she asked, "But where are Mother and Father?"

She went inside, took the lift to the penthouse. When the ornate brass elevator doors opened, Elizabeth exited the elevator and walked unhurriedly to the French phone, which rested upon an ivory table in the cream-colored lobby. She dialed 911. Moaning, distraught and incoherent, she informed the dispatcher that her parents were splayed out before her on a blood-slickened Persian carpet—that they most likely were dead—and that it seemed that their eyes had been plucked from their faces. Next, she rang the concierge and told him to expect the authorities, sprinkling her words with a few carefully inserted sniffles and sobs. And then she repaired her red lipstick and straightened her hair.

The forensics people photographed the claw marks on the deceased pair, most notably the gauges about the eyes; the eyeballs themselves were nowhere to be found. They bagged the black feathers—which were scattered all over the crime scene. There were no signs of forced entry, and the security system was in working order (the operation of the penthouse elevator required the use of a special key). Elizabeth, everyone noted, was holding up well, under the circumstances. She was now the sole proprietor of Top of the Mountain and its expansive timbered acreage.

When the press and the police had departed the yellow-tape-bordered scene, Elizabeth wandered out into the courtyard. The paving stones, Italianate wrought iron furniture, and English roses were invisible, shrouded beneath a weighty deposit of snow which glistened in the moonlight, and the only footprints to be seen were her own. Soon, a strange man dressed in a sable overcoat and wrapped in a muffler of ebony silk emerged from a curtain of whirling snowflakes. His eyes were like fire. Elizabeth went to him, and he enfolded her in his arms. He pressed his lips to hers—and her delicate fingers grew long, their manicured nails stretching themselves into talons. With the nails of one hand, she sliced her arm and then watched her red blood dribble onto the virginal snow. Her demon lover kissed the blood from her arm, murmuring into her ear,

"The mountain must be fed, High Priestess. Daughter. Hot, red blood shall fertilize the altar. Blood for the Great Unseen. Steaming, crimson blood red on white snow. Blood for the mountain. Red on white snow."

When the fiend had done ravishing her, Elizabeth re-entered to the lodge. The unmarred snow of the courtyard bore no trace of her seduction, blood and footprints having vanished. Facing the icy disk in the black, star-flecked sky, the High Priestess raised her arms—they had become great, black-feathered wings.

As icy fear began to paralyze his body, stop his thoughts, Carter threw the file onto the ground and picked up the next-to-last.

The Cat of Black Mountain

"Won't you just look at that beautiful cat," said Joanna. "He's been sleeping under the porch all week, and he devours everything we put in front of him. I think he's a stray."

"I hope somebody feeds him when we've gone home. I feel so bad, abandoning him like this, with winter coming on," responded Danielle. "I think we're the last ones to leave."

When the leaves started to fall, the tourists departed—except for the ski set, and they stayed at the lodge atop Black Mountain. Pine Rest Cozy Log Cabins was shuttering for the season. Heavy snows would inter the lodgings at the base of the mountain, sometimes entombing them until the spring thaw, which would leave them that much more mildewy than the year before. By year's end the lower terrain at the foot of the craggy mountain would be a desert of snow and ice.

"I'm afraid we're just going to have to take him home with us."

"I hope the other students in the dorm don't fuss. I'm certain I can get around the regs by asking my doctor to write a prescription for a companion animal."

"Say, Danny, what'll we call him? He's cute and cuddly, sleek and muscular—a regular macho tomcat. But his eyes—"

"Satan is what I think of when I look into those almond eyes—such a deep green with flecks of gold, set against all that thick, sleek ebony fur."

"Really? I agree those eyes are intense. They seem to know a lot that they're not saying. He's too adorable to be evil, though."

"What do you think of Prince, Joanna—as in Prince of Darkness?"

"I can go with that."

"We always knew we'd meet our prince."

"But we didn't know he'd have four legs and a tail."

"You know, this turn our conversation has taken brings to mind the Putnam County murders a couple of years ago. Remember, the retired couple, the girl who worked nights at the lodge on the mountain? Don't forget, this *is* Putnam County."

Danielle nodded.

Danielle and Joanna were roommates at Salem University, both majoring in history, with a focus on the colonial period. They had been best friends ever since kindergarten, when they had cut vampire bats out of construction paper with safety scissors, back home in Philadelphia, and they had not wanted to separate for college. As a going-away celebration, their families had rented a pair of cabins for the two weeks preceding the start of the fall term. Following fourteen days of hiking in the shadowy forest, blackening marshmallows over burning branches, and scorching meals on a pair of rusty grills affixed in the yards in front of the cabins, parents and siblings had departed the day before, leaving the coeds to drive themselves to school in Joanna's new car, her graduation gift from her proud parents.

They found a cardboard box in one of the closets and fashioned it into a carrier for Prince. After packing the rear of the SUV with their suitcases and their new pet, they returned to the cabin to lock the door.

"Oh, God!"

Joanna came running to Danielle's side.

"How horrible!" she cried.

A bluejay lay before the door, its wings fully spread—torn open from throat to tail, its entrails drawn out into the grass, a ring of crimson around the little corpse.

"That wasn't here when we left the cabin," said Danielle. "Do you suppose Prince—"

"Well, he's going to be a housecat from now on," responded Joanna. "Let's get going."

By late afternoon they were hanging their clothes in the closets and their pictures on the walls of their collegiate residence. They made their beds with the coordinated linens they had selected together, assembled their bookcase, and arranged their textbooks on the shelves. En route to Salem, they had stopped at a discount store to purchase a bed, a litter box, bowls, and a carrier for Prince. When they had completed the business of moving in, they kissed Prince goodbye and locked him in their room. They were headed to a welcome reception at the Rathskeller.

"Well, if it isn't the dynamic duo," a voice called from across the room. A head of big, blonde, curly hair glided across the room; it was attached to the neck of a young woman named Jenny. "Funny the three of us ending up at the same college."

"Yes, funny," said Joanna.

"How are you?" asked Danielle.

"Fantastic, as usual, especially with all the good-looking options in this bar. You know I can't help attracting them."

"We know you," answered Joanna.

"I sure hope you haven't any hard feelings about Ron—it's not my fault if they find me fascinating. I'll be studying theater, developing my natural talents— *Atchoo!*"

"Gesundheit," said Danielle.

"I'll bet it's that cat—Bill Redmond, the football player leaning on the bar"—she nodded in his direction—"he said he saw you bringing a cat into your room. You probably have hair all over your clothes. I'm allergic. I'll have to speak to the building supervisor about it."

"Our cat's not going anywhere. My doctor's sending a note that I need to have him for my peace of mind," said Danielle.

"Oh, it's a mental problem," cooed Jenny. "I'm not surprised."

Joanna pulled her friend away to prevent a cat fight, for Danielle had turned a fiery red. She steered her toward the hors d'ouevre trays and punch bowl.

"Someday she'll get hers," fumed Danielle.

"There's always karma," agreed Joanna.

Before long a group of freshman guys had stationed themselves by the buffet and introductions were made all around. As the roommates walked back to the dorm, they agreed that it had been a successful first night at college, that they had met some new friends.

Before they made it inside the dorm, though, Jenny came rushing down the sidewalk toward Danielle—slapped her face and rained blows upon her chest—

"You bitch! I know you did it. You're sick. You're going to pay."

One of the students in the courtyard called security, and several more rushed to pry Jenny from Danielle.

When the security guard arrived, he questioned Jenny as to why she had attacked Danielle.

"She killed my bird—she tore my canary apart! It was in its cage, in my room in the sorority house—now it's in pieces all over the room. She's psycho, man. Who would do that to a bird?"

There were plenty of witnesses who placed Joanna and Danielle at the Welcome Reception and who could verify that they had walked straight from there along the path through the campus that led to their dorm. When at last they were back in their room, they discussed Jenny's crazy behavior. The girl had always been a narcissist and a bully, but tonight she seemed to have gone off her rocker. While Danielle showered, Joanna got into bed, Prince snuggling beside her. She scratched his noble black head, the gentle mound between his perfect little ears, and the purring feline rubbed his velvet cheek against the back of her hand. That was when Joanna noticed the yellow feather stuck in his teeth.

Of course, he could not have gotten out of the room while we were out. The door was locked when we got back. Joanna threw the covers and the cat aside and rose to check the window—it was locked, too. *Just a crazy coincidence. Really weird.* She returned to bed and was soon asleep.

Prince was a remarkable cat. He quickly endeared himself to both girls, even allowing them to walk him on a leash. As a companion animal, he sometimes went to class with Danielle.

In the fourth week of Statistics class, when the professor handed back the pop quizzes from the previous Friday, Joanna was delighted to receive a grade of one hundred percent, but Danielle, crestfallen, received only a D minus. When she compared her Scantron answer sheet with Joanna's she realized what the problem was: she had misnumbered her answers, filling in the circle for question 1 on the line marked "2," and so on down the line—that was why almost all her answers were wrong! If she had used the right lines, she would have had a perfect score, too.

The girls brought their answer sheets to the professor and explained the problem to him.

"Young ladies, I am sorry, but I do not see how I could possibly use that explanation (right or wrong) to award an A to a D test. The best I can do is to advise you to check your answers carefully in future, to avoid a similar mistake."

He was immovable.

Danielle said they should drop Prince at home and then grab a beer at the Rathskeller: she was furious and needed to decompress. Joanna said that it was Taco Night, so they should eat dinner there—they could stay in and hit the books tomorrow night. Prince was duly locked in for the night. This time, Joanna double-checked the door and the window, and the old friends walked to the scholars' lair.

At a corner table in the dark lounge they laid waste to the rice, beans, lettuce, and crunchy shells; worked their way through a pitcher of beer; and discussed the mystifying aspects of the church-governments of the Puritans and the Pilgrims of colonial Massachusetts. By the time they were ready to return home, Danielle had forgotten all about her flubbed first quiz.

As they walked toward the exit, they encountered a group of students blocking the door. Danielle started to say, "Excuse us," and to move around them, but she stopped when she heard what they were talking about.

"His eyes were clawed out—his face was practically shredded!"

It did not take the young women long to realize the students were talking about their Statistics instructor. On his way home from school he had been savagely attacked in the parking lot, and he was in the hospital now.

On their way back to the dorm, the girls walked by the parking lot where their teacher had been attacked. Several cruisers were on site, and yellow tape closed the lot to residents and commuters. As the girls stood silently, watching the law at work, Joanna looked down at her feet and noticed red pawprints—a cat's pawprints. A cat had walked through the carnage and tracked blood from the crime scene. She tapped Danielle on the arm and pointed to the ground.

Danielle gasped. "Poor kitty. I hope he was not traumatized by the sight."

They wearied of watching and walked home. Prince met them at the door, leapt into Danielle's arms, nuzzled her face.

"What's that on your face, Danny?" asked Joanna, for she had noticed a reddened area.

Danielle went into the bathroom and looked in the mirror.

"It looks like blood. Maybe Prince scratched me and I didn't notice."

Wetting a washcloth, she dabbed at her cheek. The red color washed off, and her skin seemed intact, with no cuts or scratches.

"I think it *is* blood—but it's not mine."

She checked Prince for injuries and found none; and yet, some sticky red substance adhered to his luxurious fur coat and his four little paws. When she released her pal, he began to groom himself vigorously.

"What is that red stuff on him?" she asked Joanna.

Joanna told her of the yellow feather.

In their second semester they were enrolled in a seminar on the Salem Witch Trials; and each was writing a research paper examining the horrific phenomenon from a different angle. As well as being smart and hard-working, the girls were friendly and attractive, and they dressed well, so it is no wonder they soon became popular on campus. Having been friends since kindergarten, they shared most of the same interests, the same preferences for food, and the same taste in men.

It was that last which would led to problems.

The girls had a number of admirers, and they were happy for each other. It was unfortunate that they both preferred the same young man—an English major named Brad, whom they had met in American Literature 201. They had argued over the merits and flaws and the profound wisdom and compassion of *The Scarlet Letter*, after which the three had become inseparable. When spring came, Brad asked Joanna to the dance: it had never occurred to him that Danielle had been absolutely positive that he preferred herself to her friend. The night on which the invitation was proffered and accepted, Danielle pleaded a headache and stayed in to watch TV, while Joanna went with Brad to the Rathskeller.

Danielle was devastated—for she had really cherished strong feelings for Brad, feelings she had not confessed to anyone—and she cried into her pillow, scarcely aware of Prince kneading her arm with his little feet, lightly pricking her skin with his tiny claws, and purring extra loudly by way of offering comfort to his special friend. At length Danielle swallowed a sleeping pill that her mother had sent with her—in case of an insomniac emergency—with a large draught of beer.

"Danielle—open up! Open the door!" She was rudely roused from her sleep.

"Danielle—open the door! It's the police!"

She rose from her bed, groggy, felt for her bathrobe, and walked unsteadily to the door.

"Who is it? What do you want?" she asked.

"It's the police. Please open the door."

She drew the door open and found two uniformed men standing there, along with the dorm supervisor and a gaggle of students.

"Let the officers in, honey," said Marty, the supervisor, edging past the policemen to enter the room. Putting her arm around Danielle, she guided her to the bed.

"What are you looking for, dear?" Marty asked.

"My cat—don't let him out, please. Shut the door, please."

Prince was not in sight.

"He's probably hiding, with all the commotion," said Marty.

"What's this all about?" asked Danielle.

An officer stepped forward. Removed his hat.

"I'm sorry to bring you bad news."

"My parents? Joanna?" Danielle cried.

"It's Joanna. We are so sorry. She was killed tonight, and we need to ask you some questions."

"How—how—did she die? What happened?"

"Some witnesses said she left the Rathskeller with a friend on his motorcycle. They swear a black cat ran across their path. The cycle swerved. They hit a Brinks truck. Instant death. Blood sprayed all over the road. Truck driver unharmed."

"Oh, my God!" Danielle screamed, burying her face in the supervisor's shoulder. Marty held her tight as she could until her sobbing subsided.

The policemen obtained details about the relationships among the friends, the events of the evening, and Joanna's next of kin. They said that they would return in the morning to talk more, after Danielle had had some rest.

When everyone had cleared out, Danielle phoned Joanna's parents. Following a brief, torturous conversation, Danielle poured another pill from the bottle, swigged a bottle of beer, and lay down in her bed. Unable to summon sleep, she was staring at the ceiling when a movement to the left caused her to turn her head.

Prince was sitting on the window sill. The window was opened, letting in the cool night breeze.

The window had been shut and locked. I know it was locked.

The Black Mountain cat sprang from the window sill onto the bed, cozied up to Danielle's breast, and licked her face.

He was purring loud as any cat can purr.

Terror wrapped its icy fingers around Danielle's heart.

Obviously, it had been a mistake to come here. This wasn't just a brain-washed cult of Jim Jones's zombies, but a locus of evil magic. The real deal. He had walked right into it.

Carter knew he had probably been seen already. He checked his firearm, put it within easy reach. It was too dark to find his way down the mountain. He would just stay put, make no noise, and begin a retreat at dawn. If I'm still alive at dawn.

He opened the remaining file, the one that had no name:

Ambridge Carter started up the steep mountain, forging a path through the old-growth trees and tangled brush. He had secreted his car within a dense copse of trees, taking care to throw some fir-tree branches on the hood and trunk, and then hiked away from the road, the only road, as far as he was aware, up Black Mountain. As he dug the toe of his boot into the soil and looked for branches to hold onto, he began his ascent of the mist-covered mountain . . .

It came as no surprise when Carter heard the voices in the darkness

151

beyond his shelter chanting, "The mountain must have blood." He looked up from the manuscript—to see black-robed figures carrying torches. They were walking toward him.

"The mountain, Carter," a voice called from the darkness.

The mountain began to tremble. Hundreds of unseen birds cawed. Carter placed the barrel of his gun into his mouth, pulled the trigger.

The Apt Pupil of Black Mountain

What else could I have done? You tell me. Don't get so agitated—
you'll upset Cat. See how she's kneading my skirt, nestling in its
folds. You tell me—what else could I have done?
What else can I do? Remember when I first sang,

Magister, teach me. I burn to learn.
Flames leap in my core,
Fire rages in my veins,
I am alight.
Cool my desire with nightmare whispers from your lips.

Magister, teach me loathsome secrets,
Nightmare knowledge from dank
Charnel soil, miserable blasphemies out of
Forgotten catacombs
Tenant abandoned.

Magister, teach me. In a black cauldron glowing red
Meld two into one
Hideous thing. The incantation
Graven in your mind,
Teach it me, Magister.

You used to love my voice. At least you said you did. Do I still sing like a nightingale?

Dark aeons have passed since then. I am old now. But I think often of my childhood in the shadow of the dread Black Mountain. My mother and her hulking man kept the lopsided tavern with the strange obtuse corners at Bide-a-While. I shuddered at the drums that beat at night, the screams in the dark, the splatters of blood discernable on the trees in the uncaring light of day, and I would sleep with the burlap scrap which did for a blanket over my head. (I've told you all this before, but I'll tell you again, seeing how you have all the time in the world to listen.)

I would huddle in the old, misshapen manger, where, through the gaps in the roof, the sun would enter and rest itself upon an old leather trunk, which held the world within its battered frame. At first, I didn't know what to make of the contents, for I had never seen books before. Books they were, eldritch tomes—I learned new words like *eldritch*, for somehow I taught myself to read the books.

"Diabolical" and "hellish" entered my vocabulary, too. My unwatered mind drank deeply of civilizations long dead, gulped mouthfuls of worlds not yet discovered, quenched its hunger and thirst with lore of gods and alien fiends which hover near and yet beyond sight. I understood what was meant when I heard the shrieks in the night and the blackhoods chanting, "The Mountain must have blood." I joined the frenzied dances in the wood when the altar was fed with blood. Yet, all my newfound learning did not satisfy me. I hungered for more.

I wanted to learn of men and women, as well as other creatures of the world. Of art, of poetry, of song, science, stars, and the sea—in short, of everything. I had, though, exhausted the resources of my trunk library, and my mind idled again against inclination, imprisoned by the bars of ignorance.

My mother died. I still hear her screams as merely one melody in a fiendish roundelay sung by the black-robed chanters. I saw her blood upon the earth by morning light. Her hulking man ripped me from my bower, put me in her place, nearly tore me open with his rough usage. I killed him with the wood-axe in the night. What else was I to do? I had no choice but to repay him in kind.

You grow restless, but I shall go on. I sheltered within the hollow trunk of an ancient tree which grew almost to the sun, it seemed to me from below. I lived within a little room within the tree, and Cat came to live with me there. We ate mushrooms and berries and lapped up the clear water flowing in streams down the mountain. I wished—not for the people I had left behind—but for more learning. My mind demanded its due, but I had nothing to feed it save intercourse with the natural world on the mountain and conversations with Cat. And then you came.

You were seeking the tail-feathers of an owl for a spell you were working, but you found me. I was young, and you were lecherous, but I thought you were only a youth.

Nothing to say to your Lady Love, my lord? See how Cat leaps to the window, sits on the sill grooming her whiskerless face. Has she got your tongue, is that why you're silent? I'll sing for you again—

Magister, teach me. I burn to learn.
Flames leap in my core,
Fire rages in my veins,
I am alight.
Cool my desire with nightmare whispers from your lips.

Magister, teach me loathsome secrets,
Nightmare knowledge from dank
Charnel soil, miserable blasphemies out of
Forgotten catacombs
Tenant abandoned.

Magister, teach me. In a black cauldron glowing red
Meld two into one
Hideous thing. The incantation
Graven in your mind,
Teach it me, Magister.

In truth, it is a crone's voice now. Everything passes, but the Mountain itself. Yes, I dined on mushrooms and berries during my sojourn in the tree. But all the sweet fruits of nature could not satisfy my hunger for learning. Once I knew the sensual luxury of an expanding intellect, of the joys that come with nurturing the interior self, I craved more knowledge for my mind. I desired to create for myself a self that I admired. My anger at my deprivation knew no bounds, I breathed rage into my being and exhaled it out of my mind. I counted my life wasting breath by breath.

You fed my soul, Magister. What is more, I tasted the ecstasy which forbidden discourse with a learned master yields. With velvet and sandpaper you caressed my brain, and I abandoned my whole self to the touch of your mind.

Why so silent, husband? This is not like you? Cat got your tongue? Look how she leaps from my lap to the window. I shall sing to her:

Magister, teach me. I burn to learn.
Flames leap in my core,
Fire rages in my veins,
I am alight.
Cool my desire with nightmare whispers from your lips.

Magister, teach me loathsome secrets,
Nightmare knowledge from dank
Charnel soil, miserable blasphemies out of
Forgotten catacombs
Tenant abandoned.

Magister, teach me. In a black cauldron glowing red
Meld two into one
Hideous thing. The incantation
Graven in your mind,
Teach it me, Magister.

Ah, those years living in the tree. I rejoiced in the summer when I could bathe in the streams. I foraged for edible plants to stock my larder, being forced to hide in the tree during cold winter blizzards and spring thunderstorms, Cat and I curled up together giving strength to one another. Flesh and spirit knew naught but pain, and my pain fed my anger.

You were foraging in the wood one day, for an owl's tailfeather you needed for a spell you were working against an enemy. Cat saw you first (she arched her back and hissed), and then I watched you, crouching behind a boysenberry bush so you would not see me. I was not careful enough, for you saw me there.

You smiled and beckoned to me. You held out a loaf of brown bread, some cheese, and an apple. I should have run, but I had not seen such dainties for such a long time. I tried to snatch them from you, but you used sweet words and coaxed me to stay. I saw that you were a learned man— Oh, how I wanted what stores you possessed in your mind. I wanted to know what you knew with all my being. I was seduced with bread and words.

You were my very first teacher, Magister. I loved you for giving me of your learning. You knew I adored you. You had probably enjoyed the crushes of appreciative students before my time, but I did not know that then. You taught me all the knowledge of this world and not of this world. From you I received rapture— the glory and ecstasy of an imprisoned intellect newly opened, of unknown realms laid open at my feet, the veil parted, the music of the gods before the universe existed, the soul of the Void, all mine. Yet, I lusted for more.

From you I learned the blasphemies of the iniquitous texts of Al Ahazred and the invocations of Friedrich von Junzt. You demonstrated your own prestidigitorial ability by predicting floods weeks before they happened and your thaumaturgical expertise when you raised a snowstorm on a sunny day and when you slayed my dead mother's hulking man a second time, by impaling a doll made of twigs with a pin, thereby dooming him to perpetually experience in the present tense his own execution by his victim. I spat upon it. I counted his murder as proof that you returned my affection. I counted my enslaved soul redeemed. With a quill upon the back of an old fragment of parchment, I wrote "Eager Pupil" as a testament of my love for you. Cat looks at me to say that she wishes me to sing my lay again.

> Magister, teach me. I burn to learn.
> Flames leap in my core,
> Fire rages in my veins,
> I am alight.
> Cool my desire with nightmare whispers from your lips.
>
> Magister, teach me loathsome secrets,
> Nightmare knowledge from dank
> Charnel soil, miserable blasphemies out of
> Forgotten catacombs
> Tenant abandoned.
>
> Magister, teach me. In a black cauldron glowing red
> Meld two into one
> Hideous thing. The incantation
> Graven in your mind,
> Teach it me, Magister.

Note how Cat watches as I turn the pages of my grimoire. Within these pages is the story of my journey from forced ignorance into knowing, of my lessons in the histories of the globe and the stars, of the ways of men around the planet and of the beings which exist beyond the senses. Within these pages is the story of my love for you and how I became your wife. I shall read to you from them, 'though they are blurred with dried tears:

"Cat," I cried, "you fuss unduly. I am at my books. Calm yourself and sit upon my table, so that we may look upon each other as I study. Stop, Cat, you distract me. Oh, as you wish, I will follow. Why do you hiss at the crystal ball—Oh, Cat!"

The vision in the crystal led me to a cave three-quarters of the way up the mountain. My husband-teacher, the crystal indicated, was in that cave, and I did find him there. Secreting myself within a crevice in the cave wall, the nesting-place of sleeping bats, I listened to him promise me to the Lady of the Mountain. I was to be the next offering to the mountain god. "The Moutain must have blood," they always said.

The Lady lifted her black veil to reveal her bounteous locks of gold, and my husband grasped her lithe form to his own and tasted of her red lips. He vowed to teach me my true worth—as blood-fertilizer for the altar. He laughed at my ignorant pretentions to learning. With much love prattle, he undressed the lady and then himself and lay with her, while I cursed him in silence and bit my lip so that my blood streamed down my chin and dropped upon my breast.

Cat and I returned to our high house on the crag, which had also been my perfidious husband's house, to which he brought me as a bride. Next day, when he returned, I pled an earnest desire to walk to the valley, saying I would be back by nightfall. Cat and I, however, merely re-entered by the back door and hid ourselves in a crawlspace, from which place we observed the faithless wizard working a spell against me. He read aloud from a parchment, which he held over a fire burning within a black cauldron. In a triumphant voice he read that he would roast my heart and sprinkle my blood unto the earth to fertilize the altar of the Great Unseen. He cried, "The Mountain must have blood. Blood unto blood. Blood for the mountain god!"

Valiant Cat leapt from our hiding place and seized the parchment in her teeth. My betrayer tried to grab the feline and toss her in the flames, but Cat leapt out the window carrying the parchment to our hollowed tree home. When I joined her there, I saw that her paws were singed and her whiskers burned away; and, yet, she held her tail high and purred to see me.

Hear her purr now, husband. I have proved to be a more apt pupil than you thought, I think, for when you came after me, I bound you in a spiders' web that stretched from tree to tree to tree. Your damned parchment I threw into a cauldron of bubbling condors' blood, and into that I spat my hatred.

Husband, taste the burning elixir!

What, you do not relish a chalice of the burning blood flung upon your face? You do not appreciate the diabolical delicacy of my spell-casting? *I* deem my style comely, husband. Alas, I think your countenance shall no longer be pleasing to women. Worry not, though, for it is a short-lived penalty you shall pay. What else could I have done?

Do you hear it yet? Perhaps the fiery fluid has burned your ears as well as your eyes. Many wings are flapping in the distant sky, yet drawing near to this house at the top of a crag on Black Mountain. I hear the flutter of thousands of blue-violet feathers and the shrieks of thousands of sharp-beaked maws.

What is to happen to you (you would probably inquire had your lips had not been scalded by boiling blood)? You shall be dropt by the winged night-bird into a flaming volcanic crater on the far side of Black Mountain.

Why protest, husband, when you know well that the Mountain

must have blood. Blood unto the mountain. Drench the altar with fertilizing blood—but not necessarily mine.

Well, Cat, dost thou like my inditing? You have been very patient as I read to you the story of my grimoire. I count your silence and the rumbling of your belly for approval of my text. You are a good catkin, and we shall always be well-devoted to one another in our own pretty house on Brazen Mountain that glows red in the sunset in the northern territories of Quebec and looks with scorn upon Black Mountain.

The Faithless Lover of Black Mountain

To put it in simple terms, Claire was restless and bored. Not only was she a well-travelled lady—which is to say, one could spin a globe and wherever it came to a stop she had been there, but also that she had partaken of so many strange dishes that she did not know what to consider exotic anymore, and she had admired so many inscrutable relics in so many hidden corners of the world that she was just jaded. She selected her wardrobes from the runway and new automobiles on whims. Her portfolio included deeds to houses in four states and six countries, some of which she had stayed at only once, for a month or two, before abandoning them to the staff. She had enjoyed several lovers, men who had rendered life agreeable for a time, and numerous men and women among her acquaintances styled themselves her friends; they were all alike, though. Having a penchant for fine literature, she had amassed an extensive library; but, although she had wallowed voluptuously through these books on-and-off for a decade she eventually lost interest in reading, craving a novel passion—in real life, as opposed to in books—something to reignite her zest for life. Ennui was the only problem in her charmed life.

Having drained the Bordeaux in her glass, Claire twirled the crystal goblet between her fingers, willing its infinitely replicating prisms to draw her down into some unfathomable and hitherto uncharted realm. *What is the point of a person's existence,* she sighed, awash in melancholia. *What must one do or obtain in order to feel satisfied? Is there an end goal? All that is (or was or will be)—is it all just random, merely absolutely senseless? Are we—am I—no more than accidental globs of subatomic units which somehow adhere together, in configurations dictated by chance alone, for a time, only to break apart again in an endless, ungovernable, and unfeeling universe?* The idea of pointlessness was as disheartening to Claire as impermanence or superfluity. She wanted more.

Seth, she fervently hoped was at least part of the answer to her mounting discontent, would distract her, in some measure, from the existential depression which loomed so heavily. He was a good man, a self-made man—he had drive, intelligence, and wealth he was not born with but had earned. Whenever he told her that he adored her, he spoke with such unaffectedness of tone and gentle consideration that when Claire looked into his flecked brown eyes she felt cherished—and that made her feel necessary, as well. They had met in an ancient temple in Tibet eighteen months previously, and they had become engaged three months after. Until very recently, they had been inseparable. Wanting purpose most of all, Claire implored the great void in the sky that the two of them would fill the vacuum in each other's souls, a small something in the meaningless void. What is more, Claire felt strangely confident that Seth would change her life for the better.

Leaning into the snow-white velvet *chaise longue*, which was positioned before a vast wall of glass, she looked up at the radiant and silvery stars which were strewn by some legendary deity across the blackness. Her highland château was constructed nearly entirely of glass and poised upon a slender promontory that projected outward from the mountain into the ebony abyss. The daytime view from the living room window included the sable shadows and dismal recesses of Black Mountain, whose lofty pinnacle was white with snow all the year and often veiled by a tantalizing mist. Claire would sometimes speculate about just what mysterious workings went on in those caverns and crevices, and at the ski lodge on the summit, too, for inevitably the clouds sat down upon it and cloaked that high edifice from her view. One day, she would drive all over the neighboring mountain and explore it. She debated whether to call Seth again, decided against leaving another message. Maybe they could drive up Black Mountain together.

She placed the crystal goblet she was still holding on the cocktail table and took up the old book which lay next to it. Once deeply purple, time had bleached the volume's silk binding to a reddish-burgundy, and it was marred by water stains and bereft of most of its gold leaf. Carefully opening the aged text to the page she had last read, Claire sought to lose herself in the legend of the primeval Mother-Goddess, if only to keep her mind off Seth. Intrigued by the concept of the Feminine Divine as a primal force of nature (to which novel idea the volume had introduced her), she felt a weird, illogical kinship with the Earth Mother; and, for some inexplicable reason, the thought comforted her.

Beyond the vast and tenebrous gulf that stretched between the two mountains, in the penthouse of the ski lodge on the summit of the dread Black Mountain, Elizabeth Darkner surveyed her crimson bedchamber from her many-pillowed bed. She spoke to the half-asleep man who drowsed beside her.

"Seth, sweet, tell me more about your lady friend who lives in the glass house on Silvery Mountain."

Seth rolled over onto his back, and his golden-locked lover ran her sharp, ruby-polished fingernails through the brown hair on his chest.

"*You* are my lady, High Priestess," he protested, indolently, his eyes shut.

"Come, tell me. I am curious."

"Well, my heart, I really am bored with the whole set-up now, but she won't stop calling me: my voice mail is full."

"Call her. Now."

Seth opened his eyes, a resigned look on his face, and he

reached over Elizabeth's body to retrieve his cell phone from the nightstand. Locking his eyes on his paramour's face, he spoke into the phone.

"Hi, Claire. How are you? . . . I'm sorry to have worried you, but I've been laid up with the flu . . . Yes, this is my first day out of bed in a week, I am much better . . . Man, the snow is horrible here in Philadelphia. How is the weather up there in New Hampshire? . . . Maybe we can get together next week. . . Oh, you want to drive up Black Mountain? Let me think it over . . . I'm a little tired now, honey. May I call you later? Love you, angel. Bye."

Unceremoniously, Seth let his phone fall to the floor next to the bed.

"She wants to come up Black Mountain? I'm sure that can be arranged. No—*stay awake*—tell me how my business investments are faring. You've done rather well with the funds I have given you, so far, luv."

"I don't believe you've heard a word I've said, Seth," Claire complained.

"That is untrue, Claire, you were talking about a book you were reading."

"I've been attempting to tell you that I'm really fascinated by this whole mythos that personifies the earth as Gaea—"

"Yes, I'm sure it's very interesting." He looked at his watch. "Nevertheless, I must be on my way. I really am truly sorry, dear. Now, don't look so glum, Claire. Let's plan that road trip to the big Black Mountain. I know you had your heart set on going today, but I really think I'm not yet recovered from that bad flu I had last week. After I've made a few calls, I'll call it an early night and get some rest."

With tightly pursed lips, Claire watched Seth sidle toward the door. Saying, "I don't want you to catch my flu, *mon cher*," he blew her a kiss from the other side of the room, and then he was gone. She released her breath slowly, as in a hiss. Of course, she was not buying the flu story—on the contrary, she was chagrinned to discover that she could still be as inanely starry-eyed as she had been in middle school, when she'd had a crush on her art teacher. She despised both Seth and herself; yet, the thought of returning to her previous, barren life—after having glimpsed the Shangri-La of joy and meaningfulness he had conjured so deceitfully in her mind—was so much worse than never having opened her mind to that beautiful possibility. She reviled Seth for shattering her peace, however dreary that peace may have been. Picking up the glass from which Seth had been drinking his medicinal brandy, she hurled it at the window, hurled it at Black Mountain beyond the windowpane. The crystal vessel shattered into millions of miniscule, sharp shards, barely scratching the glass.

Claire leapt back as an impervious white mass billowed up beyond her window, annihilating her view of Black Mountain and darkening her living room. She hardly heard the housekeeper—who had run into the room shouting, "Avalanche!"—over the prodigious roar which accompanied the appearance of the snow cloud. Her car, loaded earlier in the day for the now-postponed Black Mountain expedition, was waiting to take them down the mountain, the housekeeper said, and a party of skiers had perished.

Quickly pulling on their warm winter coats and snow boots, the women rushed out the front door and into the idling Land Rover. Rock missiles and branches pinged vociferously on their vehicle, and a mere hundred yards to their right an enormous wall of snow—along with the hundreds of rocks and boulders, tree trunks, and splintered buildings it had uprooted—was careening down Silvery Mountain faster than the car could negotiate the slippery road. They held their breaths, expecting to be crushed by the plummeting snow and debris before they made it off the mountain; but the road continued clear and they reached the valley safely, and in good time. Keen to phone Seth from Black Mountain, which would probably still have power, Claire instructed her driver to take them to the lodge. Seth must be sick with worry for her, she thought. Probably, he regretted his recent neglect of her.

Upon their arrival at the hotel, a veritable brigade of red-coated, brass-buttoned bellmen emerged from the double brass doors; and then, as the staff loaded Claire's bags onto three brass carts, the concierge ushered the lady and her domestics to the registration desk. With abundant commiseration and lavish sympathy, he described for them the choices in accommodation afforded by the Black Mountain Lodge. Having obtained her key to the Black Mountain V.I.P. Suite, Claire turned to follow the bellhop. That was when she saw her fiancée brandishing a bottle of champagne in one hand and lifting Elizabeth Darkner's fingers to his lips with the other. As Seth turned his head, he caught sight of Claire standing near the elevator, watching him. He smiled warmly at her, while murmuring to Elizabeth Darkner, "Did you—?"

"No, but I must take advantage of this opportunity. The mountain must be fed, you know. The mountain must have blood." The High Priestess studied the diminutive brunette and calculated the price of her parka, a couture label which she could only have gotten in the Swiss Alps.

Together, Seth and Elizabeth hastened across the expanse of the lobby to welcome Claire. Tenderly embracing his snow-wetted fiancée, Seth expressed his great relief that she was safe. Elizabeth also expressed her concern for Seth's friend and her retinue, "refugees of the avalanche," as she termed them, and proffered the hospitality of her house to her next-mountain neighbor. Claire accepted politely and held her tongue. She would wait until later to have it out with Seth.

"I see. The blonde hotelier is a friend. I'm a friend. We're all friends, is that how it is?"

Having seen enough of Black Mountain—and Seth—Claire instructed her faithful staffers to ready themselves for an early departure for Portsmouth. They left at first light. Claire's disposition was not improved by the drive; in fact, the more she thought about Seth's wanton cruelty the angrier (and sadder) she became. Having settled her retinue into a comfortable hotel in Portsmouth, and having ascertained the state of the roads on her own Silvery Mountain, Claire garbed herself for a frigid midafternoon stroll to the waterfront. The wintry coast was deserted now, for most of the natives were hibernating until the spring, when the tourist migration would begin. She needed to be alone.

She meandered the red-brick lanes of the old seaside town, barely cognizant of the twin rows of two-and-three-storey red-brick buildings which embraced the waterfront. Their long, narrow windows cast indignant glances at the threatening sky and squinted at the dark-bottomed, white-crested waves, of which Claire caught brief glimpses, as she passed by the small alleys plunging downhill from the street to the water. Lost in her unhappiness, she noticed neither the beguiling boots and handbags in the shops' windows nor the seafood restaurants, wine bars, and cafes, which were shuttered, their outdoor tables and chairs huddled together under frozen tarps as if for warmth. Bereft, forlorn, and nearly dead, Portsmouth in the midst of a January freeze mirrored the desolate landscape of Claire's heart.

I feel so much closer to the mountains and the ripples in the rivers than any people I have known, she reflected dolorously, as she gazed at the seagulls gliding overhead, borne aloft on unseen winds toward inland shelter from an approaching storm: they seemed to acknowledge her presence with graceful tipping of their wings. *I feel more as if I were a plant than a sentient being of unrealised potential; and when my heart cries out, the birds and the waves seem to hear me more than any human being ever has.* She brushed her cheek with a kid glove to wipe away a drop of rain and then realized it was a tear. *Knock it off, kiddo,* she chided herself. *It is what is. Life is a lonely thing.*

"Oh, Kitty," she gasped, surprised at the sudden appearance of a sopping white-and-toffee striped tomcat. The frizzle-whiskered feline scampered toward her, mewed softly, and then wound figure eights around and around her boots. With all the might of an off-stage Aeolus blowing out the candles on his gargantuan birthday cake, a great gust lashed the harbor, just as Claire bent down to scratch the top of the rumpled gentleman's head. Seizing the trembling animal to her breast, she backed into a nearby doorway.

Unable to withdraw her gaze from the roiling water, Claire gawked at the breakers. Like white-maned water stallions rearing on great, foaming haunches, the waves were leaping higher and higher into the rising wind; and the decibel level of the combined cacophony of the screeching wind and the cymbals-smashing and snare drum-rattling of the water pummeling the rocks on the shore exponentially exceeded the din which might be produced by herds of neighing and whinnying stampeding equines racing down the cobbled street. Still huddling in the alcove, she watched as nature unbridled its force. Hurricane squalls thrust small boats onto the shore from their moorings, and then the water began rising up the old, sloping streets. Ruefully, Claire imagined that the unfolding manifestation mirrored the storminess of her own heart, as if that aching organ had been turned inside-out and emptied into the world.

Securing the grizzled tom under her coat, she climbed to the higher streets of the old town; and then she recalled a favorite seller of rare books who operated a shop in Portsmouth—the very retailer from whom she had obtained the eldritch book she had been reading when the avalanche drove her from her glass house.

"Claire—*Oh, dear,* what has made you come out—in *this* storm?" Cecelia exclaimed, hurrying toward the icy apparition in her doorway. "Quickly—come inside. I'll help you warm up and dry off. Don't these nor'easters seem to come out of nowhere, now?"

"Good evening, Cecelia," Claire said, throwing back her hood. "Although I have been, for some time now, meaning to browse your latest acquisitions, the real reason for my dropping in *today* in this storm (*and I could not be more grateful that you are still open so late in the season*) is threefold—*Oh, here, would you please help this little fellow out for me?*" She withdrew the sodden calico bundle from her coat and handed him to the shopkeeper.

"Oh, yes, of course. Poor little guy, I'll give *you* some warm milk by the heater. *Threefold*, you say?" Cecelia bundled the wet cat in an afghan and laid him gently by the radiator.

"Yes, three disasters. First, my most recent love interest stopped returning my calls—*Oh, thank you.*" She handed Cecelia her coat, which was streaming water all over the hardwood floor. "And then, regrettably, I threw a tantrum, dashed a brandy snifter at the window, defiling a rare collectable set of Christoffel stemware, after which an avalanche drove me off the mountain. I sought shelter at the lodge atop the dread Black Mountain, where I discovered that my faithless swain had dumped me for an hotelier with substantial, er, assets. I then decamped with my loyal staff for a new haven where I could ruminate on these late developments, made the acquaintance of my little friend here, and watched, absolutely mesmerized, as Nature decided to throw a sublime tantrum of her own.

"You know, it's funny, Cecelia, but here's another queer coincidence to add to the foregoing list: the book I have been reading is the one on the Feminine Divine—the story of Gaea, the Earth Goddess, which has persisted in one form or other since prehistory—the one I bought from you last spring. And here's Mother Nature today, behaving like a miffed Queen. 'Off with her head' and so forth."

"Dear, dear, Claire. Yes, that is quite a string of coincidences. Sit here, by the heater, next to your little friend. The last time I saw you, you thought you had found the love of your life—I remember that you said you had to climb a mountain in Tibet to find him.

And just as he broke your heart (and I feel dreadfully sorry for you, my dear), an avalanche and a hurricane occurred within hours of each other. *Tsk, tsk.* You should know, Claire, that I obtained the volume of which you speak from the estate of a venerable New England whaling family lately fallen on hard times, the deceased member of which had held several confidential posts in the federal government. He was also rumored to have been descended, on the wrong side of the blanket, from an ancient Celtic family in Avebury."

"A most fascinating tale, Cecilia! Thank you, my friend, for both your sympathy and this anecdote, which will most certainly augment my enjoyment of the book."

"Poor, poor dear. I know what a broken heart feels like. I wish I had a cure for it. It pains me to see you so unhappy."

Cecelia disappeared into her office to prepare a warm repast for the shivering woman and her whiskered companion, leaving Claire alone among the bookshelves. Moving closer to the radiator, Claire picked up the sodden feline and spoke soft words to comfort him—and to comfort her own stormy heart. Unbidden tears wet her face. *God, it hurt so much.* She had really loved him—and he had seemed the answer to her emptiness. Wrapping her arms around both the cat and herself, she rocked back and forth in her chair, squeezing him so tightly that he must have been uncomfortable, yet the puss did not protest. Cecelia cracked the door to look in on her weeping friend, and then quickly closed it again, to afford Claire a few moments of privacy.

Seconds later, though, the two-storey literary edifice swayed groggily on its ancient foundation—causing the frightened bookseller to dash back into her shop, fluttering her hands.

"It's an earthquake!"

The women stared dumbly at each other.

"The hotel!" cried Claire. "Surely, they have the best shelter there. Let's go!"

"All right," answered Cecelia. Still, she did not move—she only stood, gaping at Claire.

"Come on!" Tugging at Cecelia's arm, Claire ordered her, "Hurry, Cecelia—put on your coat and boots!"

"*It's you!*" exclaimed Cecelia. "*You are doing this!* Nature is manifesting your hurt and rage. First an avalanche—and then a hurricane—and now an earthquake!"

"Don't be silly, Cecelia. *Let's go!*"

Tamely, Cecelia allowed herself to be led by the woman clutching the calico tomcat.

"What do you mean, *Gone*, Seth?"

"She checked out before we arose, Priestess. We have been sleeping late, you know," he said with a sly expression and a wink.

"Find her. I intend to spill her blood upon the altar this night. The mountain must have blood. And hers most of all." Elizabeth Darkner ran her tongue over her red lips.

So, now he has decided to call, Claire thought as she viewed the overfilled mailbox on her cell phone, Seth's number repeated over and over. She replaced the phone in her handbag. *I wonder what he wants.*

A month had passed from present tense into past since the tripartite outbursts of nature had transpired, and Claire and her staff had returned to Silvery Mountain; Tom was now part of the family. Except for minor cosmetic injury, the glass house had been spared by the avalanche, just as Cecelia's bookstore had withstood this latest in a long succession of two centuries of brutal nor'easters. Seated at a curvaceous *Louis Seize* escritoire, writing instructions for her housekeeper on a notepad regarding her next destination, Claire felt it was time to move on, to put the debacle with Seth behind her. *Where to, though?* Winter was the perfect time to visit the southern hemisphere; perhaps she should spend the season at her Argentine villa. She lifted her eyes from the paper as she envisioned the pampas, and then she glanced about the room. Spying the volume she had been reading before the avalanche erupted, she moved to the white chaise and took it up. Finding her place, she settled among the pillows and resumed her reading:

"Gaea manifests her wrath by bringing down mountains and raising the waters of the ocean; and Gaea brings forth beautiful blossoms in all of the rainbow's colors on the green hills in spring. It is good to please Gaea."

Claire recalled Cecelia's silly comment that the storminess of nature had reflected the upheavals occurring within her own heart. She also recalled that her mother had told her, when she was a little girl, that whenever she was in a bad mood it seemed to be raining.

Would relocating to a new home ease her heart, though? Seth was her last, most desperate attempt to find meaning in an hollow world. Prior to falling for him, she had owned herself cynical—but that was before he so adroitly seduced her from her defenses. Ah, like most women, she was susceptible to tender words and promises. What else was there, though, what other reason for the daily trudge through life? It was becoming ever more difficult to find amusements to assuage her fatal ennui.

"Madame," the housekeeper said as she entered the room. "Seth is here. He wants to see you."

As Claire was deciding whether to see him or not, the telephone rang—it was Cecelia. The housekeeper waited while Claire answered it.

"A murder? *Another* murder? What are you talking about—Cecelia, *Really?* . . . On Black Mountain? . . . And in the general vicinity . . . Where did you hear this? . . . Oh, that's why they call it the *dread* Black Mountain, is it? I had wondered . . . Disappearances, too? . . . Evidence of cult activity—You've been reading too many of your own books! . . . Now, dear, I do think you're going a little too far—Seth is a blackguard, cruel, in fact, but a cultist and murderer? *Now, really*! . . . All right, I'll consider what you've said and look into it further ... Yes, do keep me posted if there is any more news about the neighboring mountain ... Yes, I'll be careful."

To her housekeeper, she said, "I'm not at home."

When the housekeeper left the room, she called Cecelia back: "All right, I'll admit your news has disturbed me. Is there anyone you know of who can provide me more definite information?" She wrote down Professor David Campbell's phone number.

Campbell, Emeritus Professor of Ancient Occult Religions, his hoary voice quivering with emotion, verified what Cecelia had told her and offered additional history of the cult of Black Mountain. The Dark Unseen, he solemnly expounded, was the grisly demon-god of the mountain, and it demanded blood sacrifice from its followers. The malevolent influence of the High Priestess extended far beyond the mountain proper, he warned her. If Seth was intimate with her, Seth was implicated too.

This was the last straw. Alleged cult or no cult, Claire was ready for a showdown. Her loins girded in a chic white sheath of dupioni silk and her mother's pearls, she informed her driver that she was going to pay a call at the lodge on Black Mountain.

She was done with being unhappy. She would march into the Darkner woman's penthouse and have it out with her—all the better if Seth were there, too. As the car wound its way up the constricted mountain road, Claire rehearsed her plan, envisioned the confrontation. When they pulled up to the entrance, her driver jumped out, brushed away the officious red-coated men, opened the door for his employer, and helped her out of the vehicle himself.

Straightening her shoulders, Claire marched through the brass and glass doors, strode past the registration desk, had almost reached the bank of elevators when she saw Elizabeth Darkner and Seth seated next to each other at an elongated mahogany table in what appeared to be a conference room. She positioned herself beside the open door to listen in on their conversation.

"She wouldn't see me, Elizabeth. I'll try again. Don't worry, I can win her back."

"The mountain must have blood, Seth. I *shall not* wait while you go on bungling. If not hers, then I must find someone else whose blood will fertilize the altar this very night," breathed the High Priestess. Her arms rippled, as if they were about to grow feathers.

Claire's wrath and misery were immeasurable at this point. Fury at Sean's wanton cruelty and treachery rose in succeeding tidal waves in her heart, but an overwhelming sadness consumed her even more. How she wished the world would crumble and melt into the spaces between the stars!

The hotel rocked queasily on its foundation, and in the corridors, the vases were flung from their stands. The mountain itself roared, as Claire entered the conference room.

"Need I bring down the mountain? Shall the earth dissolve into the spaces between the stars before I find peace of mind? Shall my love be betrayed and the slayer of my heart live to spill my heart's blood, as well?"

The resounding thunder of the cracking of the hotel and the splitting of the mountain cut off the rest of her words. The High Priestess of the Dark Unseen rose from the table and advanced to meet the Goddess. She bowed her head.

"We are well met, Sister and neighbor. Black Mountain must have blood. Blood unto blood. This night, this treacherous dolt's blood shall fertilize the altar of the Great Unseen, Great Goddess."

The High Priestess depressed a button on the wall and two security officers seized a blithering Seth, who kept looking from one woman to the other, and walked him out between them.

Yes, I was right, after all, Claire reflected: *It cannot be denied that Seth has altered my life for the better.*

Inspired by Nature

Brenda had always loved woods—and the deeper and darker and more remote the wood the better. So when, the recent economic downturn had enabled her to purchase a wooded parcel at a reduced price—why, she became the lady of her own dark manor—deep in the thick old-growth forest of the Black Mountain in northern New Hampshire. Twenty miles from any town, the streams on her property flowed or trickled down from the mountain, according to the amount of rainfall. The countless tall trees' branches intertwining thickly high above her head wove a branch-and-vine lattice that permitted small glimpses only of blue sky in day, or moonlight at night. There was no clearing until she reached the end of her long, winding dirt driveway. In her wood, Brenda erected a rustic log cabin and furnished it simply and comfortably. She passed many pleasing weekends and holidays in her wood, dividing her solitary hours between reading and rambling under the trees.

She judged her sanctuary a suitably creepy lair wherein to write the ghost stories which had made her a popular author. Endowed by nature with a gift for story-telling—and with a macabre sensibility—Brenda thrilled to the gloom of the dark forest. She would often make up stories as she walked in it. A winging owl presaged doom, for instance, as it flew overhead with a mouse in its claws. The violets on the moist forest floor might be poisonous plants awaiting a wandering village girl—mayhap her swain would pluck a nosegay for his sweetheart, and they would both die for love. In no time, Brenda came to know her wood well. Once she spied a crooked and forked branch that had dried up and fallen from the high limb of a tree—only to become caught upon a lower branch; when she had tried to pull it down, she had succeeded only in breaking the end off. Neither did the high winds that oft came with the periodic nor'easters dislodge it. In her head, she wove a tale that the forked branch was a pernicious omen of death and destruction.

Thus, Brenda, weaver of frightening tales, beguiled her forest holidays in her enchanted grove on Black Mountain. Her pen and her keyboard were seldom idle, as they strove to keep pace with her imagination. She placed the end of her pen between her teeth for a moment and thought about the friends whose arrival she was anticipating for a celebration of All Hallows on the night of the morrow.

Her friends, her agent Jean and Jean's husband, Bill, were driving in from Portland the next day to listen to her read her newest story, "Young Love,"—a tale which had grown out of her musings on poisonous violets—and they were bringing a holiday repast with them. Earlier that morning she had carved a trio of Jack-o-lanterns to put in the windows and on the small porch, and she had put the wine in the refrigerator to chill. Now she was hard at work, polishing the third draft of her story. She stopped writing to scratch an itchy place on her elbow. A spider bite. *How seasonal*, she thought, *I hope the spiders made a freaky web for my party*. Brenda amended another sentence in her manuscript and then bent to scratch her ankle. Another spider bite. She made a note on her reminder pad of paper to call an exterminator the next day—*atmosphere or no atmosphere*. Absently, she brushed her cheek with the back of her hand and knocked a large, spotted black spider from her face onto the paper on the table in front of her. With a shout, she jumped from her chair, knocking her work onto the floor. She picked up a book and smashed the arachnid into a red pulp, spoiling the draft of her story (she was thinking what she might do with spider blood in one of her stories, even as she cleaned up the goo with a paper towel). When she tossed the paper into the waste can she saw dozens of baby spiders emerging from the baseboard in the kitchen. Brenda looked into the cupboard for an insecticide, which she began to apply liberally to the baseboards. There wasn't enough left in the aerosol can. When she looked up and around, she saw that the room was filling with infant spiders. She picked up her coat and went out.

Pausing outside her cabin, Brenda recollected that in the storage shed she could probably find what she needed, and she turned her steps that way. It was late in the year, and the sun was setting early, and the shadows of the forest were growing long. As she approached the double-doored tool shed, she was forced to duck—a screeching owl was flying toward her head. By a quick maneuver she was able to avoid it. Already, darkness was laying claim to the wood, and Brenda returned to her cabin with the can of insecticide. She looked up at the waning orange-red of the sky, which was filtered through the dense branches.

When she lifted her eyes to appreciate the beauty of the setting sun, Brenda was surprised to spy another forked branch hanging over the limb of another tree. After she had taken a few steps more, she observed a third forked branch suspended on another tree's bough.

She entered the cabin and doused the baseboards, dealing death to the spiders, after which she opened the doors and windows to let in the chill autumn air and let out the poisonous fumes. The night sky was rapidly changing to an inky black hue, as she replaced the insecticide can in the outbuilding and secured its double doors. Behind the canopy of the branches, a full moon glowed numinously—its beams ensnared by vegetation. As she gazed upon the taciturn moon, Brenda was astonished to behold another forked branch—dangling from the bough—of *another* tree! She looked from tree to tree—and by the fluorescence of the moon she could see that there was a forked branch suspended from a bough—*in each and every one of the trees!* Brenda spun around—and, in every direction, she could see forked branches poised on the limbs of all the trees.

She ventured a little further down the path on which she had so often walked. Milky moonlight continued to disclose tree after tree bearing forked branches among their limbs. The story weaver was becoming spooked by the fantastic premise of her own story: forked branches placed ominously on the boughs of trees to signify doom.

Brenda rushed to her cabin, locked the door, and directly tucked herself into bed, burrowing beneath the warm quilt to read. Snug in her pile of pillows and cocooned by warm blankets, she fell into a dreamless sleep.

She awoke coughing—suffocating. She gripped the edge of the mattress as the coughing racked her body. She bent over, striving to clear her lungs. She opened her eyes, but she had to close them again, for they burned so badly. She touched her face—it was hot and swollen to her fingertips. Through the slivers of inflamed eyelids, she could see the black smoke. The air was blistering. She could hear the fire—the sounds of wood crackling and falling. Her eyes swelled shut, she felt for the door. Once her hands found the door frame, she willed her burning eyes open.

A shaggy, long-haired black goat was standing before her—standing on its hind legs. Its curled black horns swayed wildly, as the goat thrashed its bewhiskered neck. It gnashed its teeth and saliva ran in gobs from its jaws. It was blocking the doorway!

Blindly, Brenda reached for the bureau—trying to steady herself. But as flames started from the wall, she was forced to withdraw her arm, and she knocked off the bureau a bottle of holy water, a housewarming gift. The blaze diminished, and the snarling beast dissolved into the smoke.

Emerging from the charred and blackened cabin, Brenda stumbled to the ground. She clutched a nearby oak tree to pull herself up, but her legs were disinclined to support her weight. She was dazed and foggy—gaseous, immaterial. The rough bark of the tree scratching her palms gave her some slight comfort—this was something solid—and she, too, was real for she could feel the tree's texture and could lean her weight upon it.

On jelly legs, she ran to her car and pulled her keys from under the floor mat. Starting the engine, she placed the car in reverse and backed it onto the driveway. She shifted into drive and depressed the accelerator. Suddenly, she turned the wheel to the left—to avoid the great pine tree that was falling into her path, right across the drive—and her front bumper hit a great oak tree. As her head hit the steering wheel, a shower of acorns fell from above. Scores of cawing crows alighted from the tree and hovered between her and the moon.

Brenda came to—pinned beneath her car, her legs trapped. She felt her pockets to find her cell phone—it was not there—she tried to determine the severity of her injuries. She was in pain, of course, but was that the extent of it? Broken bones? Paralysis? Impending death? She tried to take inventory of her body. *At least Bill and Jean will be driving by here tomorrow—I should be found by them, if I'm not able to get out of here on my own*—she tried to derive some comfort from that thought. She thought that the pain was a good sign—her legs might be okay again in the end—*pain was better than no feeling at all*. She lay trapped, tearfully trying to summon some reason to hope.

Her eyelids flew open—she raised her head—*Voices*! In the distance, in the dark wood, she could hear human voices! "Help!" she called, "I'm hurt. Please help me!" *She would be rescued*!

The increasing volume of the voices indicated that the people were coming closer. As they drew nearer, their indistinct murmuring began to sound more like chanting. Brenda continued to shout for help. She saw a group of a dozen, maybe thirteen, hooded people in long red robes approaching. Each was carrying raised high before him a forked branch. Brenda froze, horrified. Continuing their rhythmic chant—Brenda could distinguish the words "blood" and "mountain"—the cowled group encircled Brenda and the wrecked car which held her fast. The circle of hooded figures parted to reveal a black goat—a black goat walking on its hind legs and waving its curled black horns. It gnashed its teeth, and gobs of saliva were dripping down its shaggy chin.

Afterword

This Creepy Cat's stories are, like most authors', inspired by real-life experiences. Life can be pleasurable, exciting, adventure-filled, and horrific. It ends in death, though—always. Until that time, we either think about the end, or try not to think about it, in which case we fill our time with meaningful and/or pleasurable pursuits.

There are times, however, when we are forced to face the inevitable: pain, fear, loss, and death. It is the natural order of things. Unfortunately, sometimes, these dire things occur out of nature or chance—sometimes they are the result of malignant human agency. People I have found to be scarier than the most horrible monsters, demons, or deities dreamt up by horror writers. The evil among us will sacrifice their fellow earthlings in a heartbeat, if there is something in it for them.

The Black Mountain stories in this volume were inspired by my trip up the dread White Mountain in New Hampshire, which I detailed in *Creepy Cat's Macabre Travels: Prowling around Haunted Towers, Crumbling Castles, and Ghoulish Graveyards*. The chapter which describes this trip—and which is entitled "America's Stonehenge"—is included in the Appendix. The landscape is as isolated and remote in real life as in my tales. I rattled up the highest mountain in the eastern U.S. in an unheated, antique small-gauge train in a raging blizzard. Eighteen inches of snow had fallen on the mountain overnight, and power was out at the station, which was half-lit on generator-power. I felt that were the car to break down or I were to get lost in the remote country, it would be people whom I would have to watch out for, more than the wildlife. Because it was so far from everything.

I wrote *Lethal* during the COVID scare, often plugging away at it at work. Earning my typing paper and toner by working in health care, and working the usual amount of overtime, I was angry at the manipulation of the population through fear which was occurring on all sides. I was never paid for staying at home— I would have spurned a public dole, anyway, for my sense of self requires that I pay my own way through life by working for my bread. An old-fashioned work ethic, but I think it is a good thing.

At work, I saw all the rules I had been taught for infection control being broken—rules which had kept me safe through decades of interacting with people afflicted with HIV, Hepatitis, Pseudomonas, MRSA, VRE, flesh-eating bacteria, and tuberculosis. The last listed is an airborne virus, capable of floating miles on a breeze, requiring a fit-tested mask and external ventilation. The new germ on the block is another respiratory virus that is spread by droplets from sneezing or coughing—it travels only about eight feet, or "spitting distance." I had learnt all this many years before, in school and in life experiences. Yet the media pundits were sounding the alarm as if germs, sickness, and death had just been invented—misfortunes we never before had reason to expect to face in our own lives. They acted as if people should expect to live forever.

I watched the vibrant elderly shrivel into nonverbal husks, having been locked in their rooms in solitary confinement for a year. None of them were asked how they would like to spend the last year of their lives—attending a beloved grandchild's wedding, or scratching off items on their bucket lists. I watched our population withdraw from relationships with other people, unless they were people on a digital screen. Look around you and see how many people are interacting with the other people who are present—and how many people are talking on an electronic device with someone who is not present, rather than the people in their immediate environment. I shuddered as I witnessed people being taught, through fear, to believe every word that came from the mouths of the talking heads on their screens—and who were taught not to question, but to obey.

Lethal developed out of my horror at the manipulation of society and the rise of an oligarchical media and political dictatorship.Many people became content to turn their thoughts and feelings over to the glowing machines they were holding in their hands or which were propped up on their tables. Others, who would not give up their right to think for themselves, had their right to self-determination wrenched from their clutching fingers. The world had become nightmarish because people decided that no one should ever become sick or die again, and no one should have the right to decide what to do with their own lives and bodies, either. Creepy Cat believes it is better to be wrong than to be a programmed robot. That it is better to die than to exist in that mechanical state. That is better to die fighting.

The title of this volume, *Cultes de Goules* is a fictitious book which figures in H. P. Lovecraft's story, "The Haunter of the Dark."

America's Stonehenge

Salem, New Hampshire is a stone's throw from Salem, Massachusetts. One day during our Salem, Massachusetts vacation my travelling companion and I took a drive to New Hampshire and visited Bretton Woods and on our return trip, Salem, New Hampshire, to have a look at the mysterious stone formations called Stonehenge on the North American continent.

We spent a wonderful day in New Hampshire, driving northward through thick primeval forest, the roads becoming narrower as we motored farther north, the mountains coming closer, and towns becoming sparser. Sparkling streams of clear blue water running down from the White Mountains bounded the road. The leaves on all sides were golden brown, orange, and yellow. Road signs warned "Brake for Moose. It could Save Your Life. Hundreds of Collisions." It was a sunny October day, temperatures in the high forties.

We drove up the snow-capped Mount Washington, the highest mountain on the east coast of the United States, and travelled from autumn into winter as well. As we climbed the mountain to Bretton Woods, New Hampshire the road became lightly covered with snow, leaves on the roadside no longer visible under their white coating. As we continued upward, snow was falling, several inches already accumulated on the ground, and the temperature had dropped into the thirties.

At the station of the Mt. Washington Cog Railroad we found

eighteen inches of snow on the ground, and I changed from shoes into snow boots, donning earmuffs and gloves, as well, for the temperature was now in the twenties and the wind was blowing hard. The team at the observatory on the mountain's peak has nicknamed Mt. Washington the place with "the worst weather in the world." Before the Depression it had been the location of a resort for the the wealthy and elite, trains going up and down the mountain all day.

We purchased tickets for the ride up Mt. Washington, the one hundred fifty-two year old railroad taking passengers only half-way up the mountain that day, on account of the weather conditions. Sometimes they run steam trains, but today they used a diesel engine. There was no electricity in the visitors' center, power out because of the snowstorm, but they were running on backup generator power.

We chugged up the mountain in cars over fifty years old, the temperature within them in the forties, and we could see our breaths. The tracks were hardly visible, rows of metal barely revealing themselves from under a blanket of snow. Our trip was to be about ninety minutes. The skies were dark with storm clouds, the landscape all white, green pines peaking from their winter coats. We passed a man, his head and hands protruding from the snow covering the rest of him, waving and hollering. We thought he was clowning around, until the train stopped and crew got off with their shovels to unbury him. He had been clearing the snow off the tracks and had fallen into a drift from which he had not been able to extricate himself. The event was considered business as usual by the crew. The train ride up the snow-covered mountain was a fantastic experience.

We returned down the mountain, and the season changed again, autumn taking over from winter. We drove southward through woodlands, small towns appearing on the exit signs along the road slightly more frequently, as we approached Salem, New Hampshire and America's Stonehenge deep in the forest of New England.

The sign at the entrance to America's Stonehenge states that "Both radio-carbon dating (C-14) and the astronomically oriented standing stones indicate the site was constructed at least 4,000 years ago like the Stonehenge of England." We purchased a self-guided tour map and entered the thirty-acre park. The nature trail took us to the site at which two-thousand-year-old artifacts had been uncovered: an ancient wigwam and cooling rack; a re-created dug-out canoe, wigwam frame, and cooling rack are on display at the site now. The guide map points out a standing stone resembling a turtle, which it notes was once sacred to early American people. The trail continues on the Double Walled Pathway past the Watch House (a boulder thought to have been used as the wall of a building that once stood there) to the Winter Solstice Monolith, named so because of its alignment with the annual astronomical event.

Sites are marked for a partially-excavated clay deposit and fire pit indicative of pottery manufacture, a sump pit, as well as remains of other structures erected at various times over the last two centuries. The Oracle Chamber consists of Speaking Tube, Roof Opening, Seat, and Closet. The speaking tube may have had an Oz-like purpose in the projection of a disembodied voice. Here is a Running Deer Carving discovered in the 1930s. The Astronomical Viewing Platform was built in 1975 to enable visitors to view the manner in which the stones are placed for astronomical purposes. The Sacrificial Table is a large stone of over four tons, above the speaking tube, named by William Goodwin, who credited the Ancient Celts with having constructed the American Stonehenge; Goodwin is the author of *The Ruins of Great Ireland and New England*. The map marks places changes were made by excavators, vandals, and carbon-daters, as well as constructions Neolithic and post-colonial.

Largely considered a hoax actually fabricated by its owner William Goodwin in the 1930s, still some believe the ruined walls and chambers are the remnants of early Native American construction or Celtic explorers from across the Atlantic. The structures have an astronomical alignment, whoever arranged them that way. Quarrying on the property, and Goodwin's relocations of stones to what he felt were the locations they had been in before being moved in relatively recent times, render accurate archaeological investigation difficult.

America's Stonehenge has inspired television documentaries and has been linked to H. P. Lovecraft. It is a mysterious collection of stones in a forest of the northeastern United States. At worst, it is a pleasant hike along wooded paths and a scavenger hunt to locate the sites on the map; at best, it is an exercise in considering what *was* there before, and who, and what has happened to them. When driving around New England, Salem, New Hampshire is a curious byway, worth a few hours' detour from the trodden path.

The Horror of Consensus
Nineteen Eighty-Four

Despite the fact that I had read Orwell's darkly prophetic book numerous times prior to seeing the film *Nineteen Eighty-Four* (written and directed by Michael Radford, in 1984), I still count the opening scene of the movie the most horrifying sight this horror fan has ever seen: because I saw *Ourselves* as the monster on the television screen. I had never felt such despair in all my life.

The film commences in an auditorium which is resounding with the bloodlustful screams of people enthusiastically responding to the indoctrination to which they are being subjected, at an event called the *Two Minutes Hate*. This daily pep-rally, war-drum pounding brainwashing session pulverizes thousands of individual human minds into raw sludge and remakes them into identical, interchangeable parts, by passing them through the hellish engines of hatred and fear, as animal entrails through a meat grinder. One can set the volume on mute and still be appalled.

In this infamous scene, most of the people in the auditorium have willingly handed over their individual beliefs and aspirations, in exchange for the protection offered by Big Brother (Oceania is engaged in a perpetual war with somebody or other, from which people always need protecting), chanting, "Traitor! Traitor!" whenever cued. Their responses are monitored by the Thought Police, who are scattered about the arena. The majority in the crowd seem to prefer base slavery to risking their individual narratives in a world which has ever been hostile and dangerous (at any rate, they must *appear* to love their slavery, as they are being watched). Some do resist, trying to maintain their hold on their own thoughts and feelings—these heroic types are subjected to torture and re-education, a la Stalin and Mao, their minds are ground into malleable mush, and they, too, are remolded into interchangeable parts.

Big Brother employs an arsenal of techniques to exterminate individual thought. For instance, History is continuously being re-written in *Nineteen Eighty-Four,* in the Ministry of Truth (this is the job of the protagonist), and evidence of a different past is incinerated in a "Memory Hole" furnace to prevent fact-checking. (Historical revision has long been a favorite tool of totalitarian societies, and one which is being increasingly used in our time, as a means of allowing the expression of once-disenfranchised voices; while the motive may be good, there is danger in pretending that the past has never happened, or in pretending that it happened differently. At this point, there is no longer any concept of Truth.)

On another front, a forward-thinking committee of the Ingsoc party is studying how to wipe out orgasm, which is dangerous to the state (in *Nineteen Eighty-Four,* babies are made by artificial insemination), for orgasm encourages the bonding between sex partners and their offspring (families). One or two people who are alone together may conceive ideas as well as babies, and ideas are the greatest threat to a totalitarian state. Today, we are being dunned with propaganda like "We are all in this together," a different way of destroying the concepts of self and of individualism. We have been involuntarily drafted into Big Brother's social army, instead of freely choosing the groups of which we would like to be members.

Everywhere one goes in Oceania, telescreens are showing war footage and mug shots of enemies of the state, and blaring the slogans of Big Brother. It is difficult for a person even to think when being dunned repeatedly by the same propaganda. Submission of the individual will, desire, thought, belief, and enterprise to the corporate whole—that is the message droned over and over again—as in our time we are constantly bombarded with "Mask Up," "Wash Your Hands," and "Social Distancing." In *Nineteen Eighty-Four*, the speakers drone on and on (and on and on . . .) enumerating production figures for the war effort from the omnipresent loudspeakers, while in 2021 we constantly hear of the latest number of virus cases.

In 2021, as in *Nineteen Eighty-Four*, only one opinion is presented in mainstream media. Other opinions, when mentioned in passing, are ridiculed, and those who express those views are labelled as enemies of the state. As in *Nineteen Eighty-Four*, divergent beliefs today are labeled "thoughtcrimes." The most frightening aspect of the current situation is the one-sidedness of the news. To my recollection, in my time, the press has never before feared a fracas, or been faced with such a dearth of conflicting opinions on any other topic. In fact, in order to increase their ratings, the press has typically tended to set people of opposing views (i.e. traditional family values v. reproductive rights) in an arena and let them have at it. We are in danger of losing our humanity, of becoming organisms which lack rational thought and free will—if we surrender our selves to the rule of the group.

What makes the human being a marvelous entity is *that which sets each one of us apart from the others*. How you *differ* from me is your glory, and the glory of our species. I love X and you hate it—how utterly fantastic! We can craft arguments and present them to one another, and be endlessly fascinated by how others' minds work differently from our own.

Many people behave as if no one ever sickened or died before 2019, and no one will ever sicken or die after the virus has become old news. But the truth is our days are numbered. We get only one chance to live our lives. We have a very long time to be dead. Are there any among us who cling to their own ideas about how they would like to spend the last year of their lives? Some people want, above all, to accomplish the items on their bucket lists; others prefer to spend their last days with their loved ones, rather than cowering in solitary confinement awaiting the Reaper.

What signifies a few more hours on this earth, if one cannot *Be*?

Citizens in a free county ought to embrace our difference, rejoice that we are not all left or right, and that both left and right are composed of an infinite array of differing opinions. The glory of the human animal is in the fact that one person is not the same as another. Think how amazing it is that one friend is Christian and another atheist—how many awesome conversations lie ahead among us. Like snowflakes, no two people are alike. That is cause for wonder. Like snowflakes, our existence is fleeting, too.

We must not allow others to think for us, for our thoughts are our selves. To permit others to reduce us to interchangeable parts in a social machine, whose ideas come down from the leader at the top (whether politician, religious leader, doctor, or social media maven), is self-murder. We must resist those who use hate and fear to goad us into relinquishing our free will. Freedom and joy can be found only by disagreeing. Our lives should be lived on our own terms and according to our own values and beliefs.

Carpe diem!

There may be no tomorrow. Let's be adventurous, and make ourselves into ourselves. Let's refuse to be ground into a common paste—to be vaporized into "Unpersons." Let's take the chances that we choose to take, risk our safety when it is worth our while. Else, the human spirit is crushed.

Be. Before you cease to be.

About the Author

Katherine Kerestman (B.A. English and History, John Carroll University; M. A. English, Case Western Reserve University) is the author of *Creepy Cat's Macabre Travels: Prowling around Haunted Towers, Crumbling Castles, and Ghoulish Graveyards* (WordCrafts Press, 2020), *Haunted House and Other Strange Tales* (Hippocampus Press, 2024), and *Lethal* (Psychotoxin Press, 2023). Furthermore, she is the Editor (with S. T. Joshi) of *The Weird Cat* (WordCrafts Press, 2023), *Shunned Houses: An Anthology of Weird Stories, Unspeakable Poems, and Impious Essays* (WordCrafts Press, 2024), and *Witches and Witchcraft* (Hippocampus Press, 2025).

More than 80 of her Lovecraftian and gothic poems, essays, and short stories have been featured in numerous anthologies, popular magazines, and academic journals. Katherine thinks *Dracula* and *Wuthering Heights* are the greatest books ever written, and she is wild about *Dark Shadows* and *Twin Peaks*. Her name is etched forevermore among the inscrutable glyphs of the Esoteric Order of Dagon and the Dracula Society.

She invites her fans to stalk her at:

www.creepycatlair.com